T0194305

A NOVEL

SOPRIS

BOOK III

ROGER COLLEY

SOPRIS
A NOVEL

iUniverse books may be ordered through booksellers or by contacting:

iUniverse
1663 Liberty Drive
Bloomington, IN 47403
www.iuniverse.com
844-349-9409

ISBN: 978-1-6632-0383-0 (sc)
ISBN: 978-1-6632-0384-7 (hc)
ISBN: 978-1-6632-0385-4 (e)

Library of Congress Control Number: 2020913468

Print information available on the last page.

iUniverse rev. date: 08/10/2020

PROLOGUE

Of issues of national and international importance, few have been as provocative during the start of the 21st century as the subject of global warming, later termed climate change. A large number of climate scientists warning of future harmful impacts were joined by a host of political leaders, the major media, and many celebrities in demanding action for dramatically reducing output of greenhouse gases such as carbon dioxide produced by the human burning of fossil fuels. Yet the general adult publics around the world placed the issue well down the scale of immediate concerns.

A handful of climate scientists would concede the average world's temperatures were slightly higher since the start of the Industrial Revolution but were skeptical that man's influence on future temperature changes would be so dramatic compared to the planet's ever changing natural variability. A few scientists believed an abrupt catastrophic warming could take place if the vast amount of greenhouse gases trapped in the frozen grounds in arctic regions were to be suddenly released. In the first novel of my trilogy, I made that abrupt warming take place. The United States was in turmoil with the population moving to safer ground in mid-America, Colorado. It later turned out a brilliant husband/wife team of Michael Reynolds and

Rose Haines saved the day with phenomenal engineering and understanding that the sudden warming was due to unusually strong activity of our source of energy – our sun, followed by its sudden return to "normal". This author's message in writing the action-suspense story *A Truthful Myth* was for all of us to keep an open mind, to listen to all sides of a debate, and accept the principle that **"science is never done, never settled"**. Myths can sometimes later become truths; truths can sometimes later become myths. This author's plea is to RAMP UP, to continue to do more and better Research into the complex field of climate science, to continue to promote new technologies that can better Adapt humans to changing climate patterns, to Mitigate adverse impacts by steadily reducing warming causes while gradually increasing mitigating technologies, and to set aside more funding to better Prepare humans for the ever happening episodes of human and natural disasters.

The second novel in the series, *In Three Days*, centers upon a terrorist issue that some may describe as science fiction, yet in reality its possibility does exist even using current technology. The key message is the American public and its leaders need to be more aware and **better prepared** in the defense of our country, the protection and security of its citizens, the number one purpose of the American governments. The attack on the United States takes place on 9/11/2021 with two weapons of mass destruction – an electromagnetic pulse bomb and a genetically modified Ebola virus that can spread airborne like a cold virus. The antagonists also send six assassins to the United States to kill top persons who just might find a way to mitigate the damage or to quickly retaliate. Again Michael and Rose are in the middle of the action. Five of the assassins are killed, but the sixth, a beautiful young Afghan girl named Fila survives. She wounds a U.S. Marine and was to kill Rose but backs off as Rose clutches her one-year old baby close. In the end, Michael and Fila save the day, but Fila is conflicted as to her innocence or guilt or to what the world is all about – is it of reason or of insanity. She wants to find a way to end violence. This 9/11/2021 story continues in this final novel, *Sopris,* the beautiful stand alone mountain in Colorado's Rocky Mountains. The novel is not one of suspense or a thriller; rather it has a very special purpose, prayerfully, inspirational.

PART I

One

September 11, 2030

On the other side of the massive desk almost completely covered with scattered papers, Alex's eyes were pleading, his jaw opening wider, his face begging for a response. His knees on his chair pushed harder, banging against the desk. Michael Reynolds sat unmoving, face stern, staring back. The boy persisted. "Com'on Dad, you promised. I'm ten years old today. You promised on my tenth birthday you would tell me the full story. Please ... now Dad."

Michael glanced down at his watch. It was only 7 o'clock. The birthday dinner for Alex went fine. It was still early. "Okay, so inquisitive you are, but you're right, a promise is a promise. You've waited a long time. Let's go sit on the couch."

The two rose in unison, moved together to a luxurious sofa, and sat down side by side, Michael turning and leaning in towards his bright young son. The large window curtains were drawn, the table lights low. The ambiance of the room was captivating and perfectly set for a telling and listening session.

So Michael began to tell the story of what happened nine years before. Alex was all ears.

━━━●◄━━━

October 11, 2021

The sound of the knocking on the door was faint, barely audible. Zachary, reclining comfortably in a large brown leather chair, lowered the book he was reading, sat up, and tried to listen more intently. There it was again – a little louder this time. From his chair, he glanced out the large living room window near the front door, but it was nearly dark now. A bright star was already twinkling in the brisk evening sky. At this time of autumn at an altitude of nearly 7000ft, chilly nights become the norm, especially high in the Rocky Mountains by the town of Basalt, Colorado.

Zachary Holmes, a handsome young man with a clear complexion and cleanly shaven, looked puzzled. The first child of George Gelayes and Colleen Holmes, Zachary was a scholarly 22 year old recent college graduate fascinated with the major religions of the world and their varying theological differences, especially after the incredible, still inexplicable, terror attack on America just a month ago. He felt relieved and fortunate that he and his family had survived so well. His mobile satellite phone had regained its reception in just a few days after 9/11, but his town's main electricity supply source remained completely shut down. Luckily, his father had recently added an emergency generator to their home, powered by full tank of diesel fuel along with an array of solar panels installed on their roof. Along with their home's nearby water supply from the Roaring Fork River and his mother's spacious vegetable and potato garden, essential family needs were being met quite adequately. Also fortunately, as he learned from news on his cell phone, the deadly virus which had been mysteriously released on 9/11 had blown easterly towards Denver, and that there was no contamination high in the mountains.

Rising from his chair and proceeding cautiously towards the front door as the soft knocking continued, he slowly opened it just a view inches. His father had taught him repeatedly that when he was home alone to be careful about strangers who might be prowlers. But this was different and unexpected. His eyes suddenly widened, his mouth dropped wide open as the inside light reflected off the face of this unknown being – for starring back at him was this complex image of bewilderment, beauty, hurt, begging – stunning green eyes, smooth tan skin, perfect features. This radiant young woman, despite her incredible physical attraction, at the same time looked completely exhausted, shivering in the cold. It was difficult to do, but Zachary somehow managed to look beyond her as he pulled the door open a little wider - she stood alone, and there was no vehicle of any kind outside to be seen.

"Please," Fila pleaded hesitantly, softly. "I … I am not to be a bother to you. I just need a rest right now… just to warm up and then I'll go on."

Zachary responded immediately, as if being commanded, opening the door wide, beckoning her in. He stuttered in his amazement. "Yes, yes … okay, please … yes, come in."

Fila slowly entered the warm room, and after a quick shiver, removed her western-styled hat, her long dark hair falling, and looked gratified to be out of the chill. She carried nothing in her hands or over her shoulder. She was dressed in a modest weight tan jacket, blue jeans, and wore low cut black boots. Zachary could sense her immediate relief from the chill outside while also sensing her near exhaustion. "You're alone?" he asked with his voice now rising. "Please, please, sit here," he offered, pointing her towards his large leather chair. He led her to the chair and motioned for her to sit. She appeared tentative and frightened as she reclined on the edge, but looked grateful with a slight smile as her eyes met his.

"I'm sorry, I don't mean to intrude. I just needed to rest for a moment out of the cold. I …."

"No, no, don't worry. No problem. Let me get you something. Some hot tea? Something to eat? " Zachary's mind was racing. *Who is this? This beauty. What is she doing here? No matter, she has come into my life. I have to help her.*

"My parents and sister are out til late tonight helping a neighbor in town who has no heat, but listen … I have some of my dinner left over. Are you hungry? Please, get comfortable; then you can tell me who you are."

"Thank you … you are very kind. Yes, some tea, fine … water … and yes, if you have some food." She looked down, as if seeming embarrassed by her predicament.

Zachary could sense his emotions exploding inside. In his 22 years he had never experienced anything like this before. This beautiful stranger with the alluring large green eyes seemed to be grabbing hold of his inner self, his emotions; irresistible, and those exotic eyes - so mysterious, but so tired. *Did she walk a million miles just to see me?*

"Let's move to the kitchen. It's warm there, and I can make us some hot tea and heat up my left overs." He wanted to take her hand but thought twice. Fila obliged by looking up with a slight smile, revealing now more of her flawless face. Her skin, her lips, her nose, her teeth – *all perfect*, Zachary thought to himself. He tried awkwardly to smile back but simply felt too much in awe as he witnessed his new discovery. Instead, he just motioned a wave and turned towards the kitchen. Fila rose and followed him. He motioned her towards a seat at the kitchen table and in quick succession filled a pot of water, lit the stove, opened the refrigerator, and pulled out some contents - all while trying to start a dialogue.

"My name is Zachary. I graduated last June from college – Regis University in Denver. Nothing as great as the National University there in Denver of course, but a very good school. It has a religious affiliation, which appealed to me. And, and well ... you, you are?"

Fila lifted her eyes to his again, but only for a brief moment. *Another nice American,* she thought. She sat silent. He waited patiently for her answer, nervously staring.

"I am so sorry to bother you. I will move on when ..."

"No, no," Zachery blurted out. "No bother at all. You know it's supposed to be unusually cold, even colder later tonight ... so where are you headed? I have a car. I can give you a lift."

"No, no," she replied, her voice rising. "That's ok. I ... " Fila seemed puzzled, lost for the right words. Similarly, a sensation of confusion enveloped the mind of Zachary. He could not place the accent in her voice or understand why she hesitated so much.

He pursued. "I notice you don't have even a little handbag of any kind. Do you have a cell phone? A satellite connection? Money? You know even my ancient parents – they are 46 and 44, are electronically bound, always looking at their emails and texts, missed calls. You know. Of course, not as much lately after this big attack on 9/11. What a disaster. Who in the world would do such a crazy thing? Especially to America – we have always been so good to the whole world ... thank goodness the virus didn't blow this way.... And my 14 year old sister – she always has that mobile in her hand."

Fila stared straight ahead, speechless. Zachary looked at her closely after his words for some kind of response. He poured hot water into the two cups with their waiting tea bags. He could sense she did not want to reveal anything about herself. He waited but still no response as she placed her two hands around the warm cup, her eyes down. But he could not give up his pursuit for answers. He would try to overwhelm her with kindness. Some psychology.

"Look, if you are in some kind of trouble, well I can help. I would be glad to. Are you a hiker with no pack? Is your car stuck somewhere? Were you set adrift by some bad guys? Are you running from home? Did you escape prison? Are you ..."

Fila finally raised her hand to stop him, finally interrupting him as she looked up at him, sensing this young man quite different than the young men of her native Afghanistan – the young rough, violent men of the Taliban. More like her former lover on the island of Dire, more like the American, Michael Reynolds, who she had spent the last month with in house arrest. *Kind,* she mused.

She thought back to her escape from violence in Afghanistan to a secret island called Dire where the people were kind and peaceful, later to her transformative willingness to follow the teachings of the island's leaders – to act upon their promise of world peace by destroying that nation ultimately responsible for all the violence in the world – the United States of America. Then to her mission to assassinate one of America's top scientists, Rose Haines, and her failure to do so with rifle raised as her target held her baby in her arms; her wounding a U.S. Marine by shooting him in the legs; finally to the dramatic conclusion with her saving the day against the ultimate villain. Other than that one evil person, every American she had personally met was kind, fair-minded. *In truth, there had been no reason to try to destroy America.* All that was back to 9/11, a month ago.

Fila continued to hold her hand up to pause Zachary. Her thoughts continued: she had escaped from her Denver house arrest with no possessions other than the hat, clothes and shoes she was wearing. Hiding in the shadows by daylight so as not to be recognized, walking in the chill of the nights almost 25 miles nonstop each night, eating snow or drinking water from the mountain streams to keep herself hydrated, crossing up and over the Continental Divide, but now her planned journey to San Francisco to escape America suddenly appeared ridiculous. *A boat to where? How do I eat? I have no money.* So at Glenwood Springs, she decided to go higher up into the mountains again. Maybe find a way to survive as a mountain person like her Afghan ancestors. But hunger and the chill finally gave her pause – a secluded home near the little town of Basalt. Although extraordinarily physically fit from her 9/11 mission training, she had never trained for the cold or facing hunger.

She looked up at Zachary who was wide-eyed standing above her two feet away. She was now more confused than ever. *Should I reveal who I am? That I am wanted? That I had been under house arrest at the same time I was being called by some a heroine? That I came to America to kill an innocent? That I backed down, but did wound a soldier, and his commanding officer wanted me in jail or hung? That I was being treated kindly and told I had a chance for a pardon by the new President of the United States? That I didn't know who to trust?*

Her hand finally dropped. She spoke up clearly. "Zachary, your name, right? Zachary, you have emergency electricity, you have a satellite cell phone, you have news. You just told me you know what happened on 9/11. You know about the six foreigners? Can you guess who I am?" Fila's eyes dropped as she hurriedly began to stuff the warmed left over lasagna into her mouth. On the one hand she prayed he did not; on the other hand, she thought *maybe I shouldn't be running away.*

The look of amazement upon Zachary's face was tumultuous. He stared intensely at her as he slowly sat down on a chair next to her. He searched for the words. "Yes, we know all about the 9/11 attack, the EMP bomb knocking out transformers, the airborne contagious Ebola virus, the six assassins - the five men dead, the lone woman captured. They said she was a beauty, bright green eyes, light brown skin…. " Zachary pushed his chair a little away, his head turning down, reflecting, pausing, speaking softly. "You, you … so you are Fila, the Afghan girl, held in house arrest at the famous Michael Reynolds' penthouse in Denver…. So they let you go or you escaped?"

September 11, 2030

"Wow, Dad. You are finally opening up to me what happened back when I was one. I have been waiting for this for so long. So when Fila escaped from our home in Denver, she made it undetected walking to Basalt. How far is that? Isn't that a little town near Aspen? And how did she escape? And why?"

Michael Reynolds, now a very handsome, well-built, mature 46 year old with ample dark hair and strong facial features, sat back on the sofa and sighed, rolling his eyes at his all too smart young son. "Alex … ok, you seem to want to know everything…. Yes, she walked some two hundred miles, only at night, little food but lots of water from streams along the way. By early October the plentiful edible berries that grow in summer along the streams were freezing, so not much nutrition there. Using small rocks she did crush some unopened pine cones to get their seeds but again not much nutrition there, just enough to walk over the mountains at night. Route 6 used to be the longest transcontinental road in America, Maine to California. From Denver it heads west over the Continental Divide, joining with and separating from Interstate 70 at times.

"She originally thought she would follow the route all the way to the west coast, but by the time she got to Glenwood Springs she realized three things: first, while there were very few cars or trucks on the road at night shortly after 9/11, she couldn't keep dodging the few that came along not wanting to be seen, and finding a place to sleep in the brush during daylight was no easy endeavor; second, from the little towns she passed along the way like Golden, Idaho Springs, Georgetown, Frisco, Avon, she could sense the United States was in still in chaos from the attack the month before, and how would she survive through our western deserts with no money, and where would she go even if she did reach the west coast; third, like your mom and me, she had quickly recovered from the virus, but what if she got it again.

"She was getting very hungry and tired, and the nights were below freezing. So she decided to become a mountain girl and left Route 6 at Glenwood Springs and started a descent up Route 82, the Roaring Fork Valley, towards Aspen. She remembered from her studying maps of Colorado at our apartment, high above Aspen near the Continental Divide was a beautiful desolate area that once served as a tent city for early miners looking for silver. And plenty of trout streams there…. But two nights later, before she even reached Aspen, she tossed it in and decided to take a chance and threw her fate to that little house – where she met Zachary."

"Ok, ok, got it. But go back," Alex interjected. "She was with us, as what - a prisoner for a month?"

"No, she was never really in captivity like a jail or anything like that, more like house arrest in our penthouse apartment. I had a double bolt lock on our door to the hall, but she did go out with your mom once in awhile. Remember, I was appointed to the presidency of our National University just a week after the 9/11 attack, so I was pretty busy during the day. Fortunately, we all strengthened our immune systems and recovered from the weakness of the virus pretty quickly. And luckily it died out quickly after killing many millions of Americans that first week. Our friend Alexis Graham had been sworn in as president of the United States shortly after I learned the assassins had murdered President Paul Jennings. She had to take command of the situation nationally, and we all had to find ways to maximize all the millions of emergency generators in the land. We had to work with the utility companies to restore power to the nation's electrical grid. It actually took years to complete the task. But the main task of immediate concern was getting enough food and water to the American citizens.

"Right, we had to provide food after the run on all our food stores. Thank God, the South American nations were unaffected by it all and immediately began to export all they could to us. Just as bad a challenge was our capability to get the word out on how to attack the contagious Ebola virus. Again, thank God the virus suddenly and quickly lost its strength to infect. Still, it has been estimated that some twenty million Americans died within a week of the attack. Did I already tell you that, Alex?"

"Yeah, all that is in our history lessons at school," Alex piped in strongly. "But Fila, and you and mom and me – why did we have her? How did we keep her? Why did she come here? Why did she leave?"

"Son, I suffered a lot of self- doubts and a lot of severe headaches thinking about all that happened during that time. It was one national crisis after another, and a fear of the future it could all happen again." Michael paused and looked away a moment. He knew Alex did not want to hear all that deep government and national security stuff. "We had three bedrooms, the master for mom and me, yours with a crib with sides – you were just learning to walk, and the third was a converted office for Fila. We brought her home with us because of all the confusion – electrical power off, the virus hitting us all but you…. In a strange way, mom and Fila were very close. Fila had been sent to kill mom because she was a brilliant scientist, and the bad guys did not want any bright Americans to figure out a way to stop the virus. But Fila couldn't pull the trigger – women's maternal empathy I guess - then she saved all of us by turning the tables on a madman about to shoot us.

"Anyway, under so called house arrest with her status under review, we locked the door at night. She was very confused. She had been led to believe America was evil. She came as an enemy. She shot and wounded a military guard, a U.S. Marine assigned to protect us, but she also saved us. She didn't know if she was going to be pardoned or punished. Mom and I made the case for a pardon. The top general in Denver wanted her handed over for treatment as an enemy combatant. It was confusing for everyone. Then one night three weeks after we had her with us, she figured out where we hid the key to the dead bolt and the next morning we discovered she was gone." Michael paused a long moment staring away. Alex was wide-eyed.

"Ok, so she walked to Basalt. But she must have told you something the time she was with you and Mom. Like, who was she really? Did she really think America was evil? Where did she come from? You must have …"

"Right. Okay, stop. I'll tell you," Michael interrupted. "She was very quiet the first week she was with us, head down a lot. She didn't seem to want to look us in the eye. Like she was ashamed. But then when mom started taking her out, she started pumping mom with a lot of questions. First about why our central government had moved to Denver during the warming crisis and how mom figured out the unusual sunbursts that caused the sudden melting of the trapped greenhouse gases in the permafrost above Canada, and how I engineered all that desalted water to get to the West and to Denver, but then their conversation turned to the way Americans live, like their personal freedoms, their choice of leaders, their civic duties, their charity.

"Finally, I could sense a softening in her. We broke her silence. By the second week with us, we sat for many evenings after a late dinner and talked. She told us of how two powerful men with access to money and weapons were tired of the world's unending violence. They fled to a deserted island off the coast of India and soon attracted tens of thousands of like-minded persons who would help them establish a peaceful society cut off from the rest of the world. But they soon felt their mission was not complete, their destiny not fulfilled. To a select few, they made known their secret plan to destroy the United States, the nation they somehow mistakenly believed was the planet's superpower devoted to unending violence. They had the access to money that could purchase a powerful atom bomb, launching platforms to put it in orbit, scientists that could genetically-engineer bacteria and viruses. The bomb, exploded high above our mid-point Kansas, would knock out all our airborne communications, and the pulse coming down to the ground would destroy our electrical grid. The deadly Ebola virus would be altered to spread like the common cold. The..."

Alex frowned. "I know, Dad. I know. We were taught all that technical stuff in school. But Fila, what about her?"

"I want to be sure you know how lucky we were. It could have been worse. Our nation was unprepared back then. The majority doesn't want to think about bad things – that's only natural – but **our government is there not just to preserve order but also to defend us. It's their duty,** he emphasized. History is replete with the violent deeds of men. Okay, so where were we? Fila ... how did she become involved in all this madness, and what's become of her the past nine years."

Alex straightened up.

Two

Late September 2021

Rose stood up from the dining table and removed the three dinner plates. Fila looked up and smiled at her. Michael looked serious. Top on his mind was that the building's emergency generator was running low on its fuel source and that candles only were to be used after dark, and that food reserves in Denver were diminishing quickly. He turned to Fila.

"Today I submitted my written report to both General Armstrong and to President Alexis Graham. I want you to know, Fila, I made the case for clemency for you. A pardon from our president would set you free, but I did propose certain conditions, like your performing certain very demanding civic duties in America for a minimum of five years. You know I cannot guarantee anything. Our military wants to see you in jail forever under what we call a 'foreign enemy combatant'.

"Our close friend, Alexis, is sympathetic. I did go into detail how after we obtained your weapons from you in the lab, that you cooperated with us in telling the story of how you attacked us, who was responsible, and the mission of you six assassins. Of course I mentioned that you voluntarily gave up your weapons to us. Most importantly, how you recognized that our so called brilliant American microbiologist Jonathan Dean was really on the side of your sponsors, that he was really the mastermind behind genetically-engineering the Ebola virus, how he murdered our university president, Richard Frost, and about to kill all of us when you grabbed your pistol from Rose's pocket and shot him clean, four times. You saved us. Our satellite communications were restored at the same time, and from Alex we had discovered the remedy for combatting the virus.... So here we are."

Rose returned to the table and sat down, staring at Fila, who put her head down and began to speak, softly, tears coming to her eyes. "Michael, Rose, thank you, thank you. I am so, so sorry. I was looking for peace and look at what has happened. I am so ashamed. I don't know what I am, what I have become. In just a few weeks you have taught me America's blessings of liberty, of kindness. Whether I ever deserve that - no, I cannot. I don't know what to think."

"Fila, dear," Rose calmly replied to her. " I think it would help all of us understand better if you told us your story ... start from the beginning -- Afghanistan."

Her foreign accent became almost negligible, no longer a factor. She could be clearly understood. She started softly at first but her voice gradually got stronger. She spoke without a pause. She seemed to be lifting a burden from her deep sense of guilt.

"I was born in a little village south of our capital city, Kabul, just after the Russians ended their ten year occupation of Afghanistan. Why they were ever there I don't know for sure, but the Islamic radical group known as the Taliban was principally responsible for driving out the Russians. I think our government originally had asked Russia to help drive out foreign disruptors, but Russia then took over, and things got so out of control that we lost a couple million people those years in the fighting. As a young girl, I was told the United States and Pakistan actually helped the Taliban and its allied tribes with access to weapons, but then I learned from my moderately religious family that the Taliban was taking over after the Russians left, which meant rule by the very strict interpretations of Islamic Sharia Law. This especially meant harsh treatment of women – no education, no liberty, bound to the home, and to the demands of men. My village and my family experienced nothing but violence resisting this harshness. I still have nightmares about it. It was horrible.

"When the Americans drove the Taliban out in 2003 while chasing those responsible for the 9/11 attack on America, Kabul was transformed. As a young teenager, I felt blessed to have found both a job and a school to go to. But ten years later when the Americans left in 2014, the Taliban and their ruthlessness returned. My friends and I lost everything. It was terrible. Two years later, I was ordered to marry an older Taliban fighter, but I think it would have been more as a sex slave. Just by pure luck, I ran into man conducting secret interviews for young people to move to an island between the Arabian Sea and the Indian Ocean. He said he liked my looks, but whatever. The whole purpose was to escape the world of constant violence and fear to an oasis of peace. It sounded too good to be true.

"Oh, am I talking too much? Should I go on?"

"No, no, we want to hear your whole story. Go on," said Michael listening intently.

"Well, I guess it was too good to be true. The leaders there preached that they were living in peace, and we were. There was no official religious doctrine to follow, no political doctrine, just grow our food, keep our places of living clean, be orderly, and help others. But soon I was introduced personally to the two founders of the movement and to some of their closest followers, one who I fell in love with, Asa, one of the group I came here with. He's, he's gone now…. " Her voice softened. Her head dropped a moment before she continued.

"I was brought into the confidential circle that a Master Plan had been developed that our little paradise was not enough. That we must also act in a way to bring peace to the entire world -- bribing the big countries into giving up their weapons. Preposterous, but like others I fell for it. Then I learned that that goal was not enough – that the powerful United States would never go for the bribe and therefore evil America would have to be destroyed. Oh, how was I ever brainwashed! I underwent intensive training. The theory put to my little group was that if America didn't receive the full blast of the EMP bomb or the full effect of the Ebola virus, that we would have to stamp out their leaders and top scientists who might combat our weapons or quickly retaliate. I was the only female of the six to be sent, but I became an expert marksman with that AK-47 and Russian pistol. I was perfectly physically fit and perfectly brainwashed. And they claimed the vaccine they gave us would make us immune to the virus. Now we know that also was a lie.

"Only they assigned me to kill a woman. I never expected that woman would be holding a baby close to her breast. I realize now how wrong we were. But for a while at first, we were so right about the desire for peace, to live without fear, without violence…. Will we ever find it? Michael, I'm so sorry I harmed you at the top of the steps. I'm so sorry I shot that soldier in the legs. I'm so glad you told me he is recovering well."

The days and evenings went on with Rose walking out of the top floor penthouse apartment and building daily, frequently with Fila at her side wearing a western hat pulled down as far as possible. Rose wanted to avoid any questions as the word was getting around about the assassins. Emergency generator sounds pierced the air on every block as the Denver citizens were learning the city's electric grid would be down for some time. Word was spreading to wear something over one's mouth to avoid the virus., drink water as much as possible and take vitamins as best they could find. Food supplies were beginning to run low while the rush continued on stocking up on vitamin C to strengthen one's immune system against the virus. Those having satellite cell phones were getting perfect reception while cell tower transmission was sporadic. Rose was amazed that resilience and purpose seemed to be the mood of the city, not panic, despite the fact that many of the initially infected with the Ebola were quietly giving up to an agonizing death. City, state, and federal officials, including the many sick and weak within their own ranks, were overwhelmed with the multiple tasks at hand, but seemed to be facing their duties with determination. Hospitals were overflowing, and there was no vaccine or antiviral for the deadly Ebola. The American scene was dire, devastating.

Each evening, upon returning from a full day's activities at the National University, Michael continued his conversations with Fila about her background in Afghanistan, the details behind the 9/11 attack, and her role in it. He seemed determined to try to understand the thinking and the motivations of the assailants behind such an incredible undertaking. Science and engineering -- the mainstays of Michael's brilliant past, but now a new dimension enters. *How are people's perceptions, their motivations, their thinking – how so different?*

Is it incomprehensible? Or is there a pattern, an answer to be discovered? Love, compassion, learning, the quest for new knowledge – yes, I have all that, but violence? Why is the history of man so full of violence? Among men and among nations. And who really is this incredible creature – this beautiful, mysterious young woman so enchanting, but so overwhelmed with contradictory thoughts and actions?

———————•———————

Fila felt so relieved one evening when the building's emergency generator failed and Michael and Rose were attending to little Alex – a pause from the constant questioning from inquisitive Michael. She picked up a lit candle from the dining room table and moved past a collection of books aligned on a living room bookcase. She noticed a book with a map of Colorado and the Western United States. Shortly after her arrival to the west coast a month ago, the subsequent trip to Denver by auto had been planned and controlled by Asa. She had no knowledge of the route, just that it seemed a thousand miles. *Maybe I should get back to the west coast and try to get back to Asia somehow. How? America is in chaos. Can I walk it? At night, so I am not recognized? I am an enemy to these people. They are so kind to me, but I should not be here. I am a burden.* It was approaching October. The weather in the Rockies would turn to winter soon. She noticed a Route 6 on the map, leading from just a few blocks away and headed all the way across the continent going west. Mountains then deserts. *They did it two hundred years ago – I can do it now.*

Three

October 11, 2021

Zachery seemed temporarily lost for words. But Fila, with her identity now revealed, had to reach a decision fast. While at first she had given her journey up from exposure to cold and hunger, her body was now warmed up with the heat of the kitchen stove and the hot tea, and finally with some real food in her stomach, her hunger was gone. *Maybe I can go on and maybe only two more nights to Independence high above Aspen where I can survive on my own if this Zachary will give me blankets, some food to hold me over and a pole and net of some sort to catch fish.*

Reality then set in. Zachary shook his head and interrupted her thoughts. "Fila, listen to me. You cannot go on. My guess is you escaped; they did not release you. You walked here from Denver. Who knows where you thought you would go, but wherever you were headed, winter will be coming. You will not survive our winter outside. Or do you have someone you are trying to see and you only stopped here first out of desperation from cold and hunger?" Fila put her eyes down. "I take it the answer is no. You are a fugitive, but maybe innocent. I heard in the news on my phone this Fila person may be pardoned by the president but it's controversial. You must be confused…. Stay here. We can take care of you until things are settled." Now it was Zachary looking with pleading, begging eyes.

"But how can I stay? Your parents? What would I do? I would be a burden."

"Nonsense, my mom is devout Catholic. She is a very empathetic person. She volunteers at our St. Vincent Catholic Church in downtown Basalt, just a mile from here. We can shelter you until things work out."

"But … ". The content bodily feelings Fila had a moment ago dissipated quickly. She had not found a quiet place to hide and sleep off the main road to Basalt that day as the Roaring Fork Valley had grown so much ever since Aspen had become a major destination ski resort back in the 1960's. The way to Basalt from Glenwood Springs, Route 82, was lined with homes and businesses. She wanted to respond to Zachary's kindness, but the kitchen warmth and full belly was now making her long for sleep. She was fatigued.

"Fila, please stand up. You can go and get some sleep in my bed, and I will take the couch in the living room. Then you can think clearly." With that, Zachary gently tugged at her arm helping her to rise and leading her past the hall bathroom with a nod for her to notice it, continued to escort her into his darkened bedroom of the one story home, and gave her a gentle push onto the bed, pulling off her boots and placing his pillow under her head. She was out before he reached out to shut the door.

———————•————

Two hours later, the front door to the home opened. George, Colleen, and 14 year old Grace entered the living room returning from a good deed they had accomplished for a neighbor a half mile walk away. The house was dark except for a nightlight in the center hallway, and to save the fuel of the emergency electrical generator, the threesome all moved to their respective bedrooms without touching a light switch, never noticing Zachary asleep on the living room sofa.

Around 8 a.m. the next morning, bathrobe clad Colleen had the coffee ready to pour as George wandered into the kitchen in jeans, a T-shirt and bare feet. The wood-burning stove there had already taken the chill out of the air.

"Morning, dear. I slept really well and didn't even hear you get up. Smells good in here," George offered.

"Yes, and lots to do today, and I will need Zach's help. Can you please wake him up."

Without a verbal response, George turned out of the kitchen, never looking into a visible living room, and down a hall to Zachary's bedroom. *Hmmm, that's strange; he never closes his door at night.*

Opening the door all the way, George hummed out "Zachary!" followed by a quick look at the bed and then a double take. Sprawled out on the bed with clothes and a jacket on was not Zach but a long dark haired … girl? Walking over closer, George could see this was not a young girl Zach's age but slightly older than Zach with very pleasant features, at least the best he could see in the dim light. He opened the window curtains to their full extent. She did not budge. He stared a moment longer at her then turned around and walked out, smiling broadly. *That son of mine. No sooner out of college than he has the women.* As he walked back towards the kitchen he noticed that the hall bathroom that Zach used was empty, so he kept walking towards the kitchen with eyes looking everywhere. And there was Zachary, stretched out on the living room sofa with both arms reaching out towards the ceiling, his eyes wide open.

"Zach, my boy. You have some explaining to do," said George, smiling and sitting down on the big lounge chair across from the startled Zachary.

"Dad! You didn't wake me when you came in last night. I was right here. I … I wanted to tell you …"

"I know. You have a girl from your college, or better yet, maybe a young pretty professor visiting and you gave her your bed to sleep in. But you didn't even let her borrow a pair of your mother's pajamas? She's still asleep on top of your bed with even her coat on."

"No, Dad. Let me explain. She knocked on the door last night … cold, tired, and hungry. She's a fugitive, but I don't think a criminal. She is the one who attacked our people in Denver, but she is no longer dangerous. We have to help her. We …"

"What!" George's face quickly turned from the congenial to one of anger. "Is she dangerous? What is she doing here? Son, we have to get the police. I've told you about drifters. This is worse. This is …"

An interruptive voice was heard. "Sir, I am sorry. I mean no harm. I will gather my shoes and go. Your son has been so helpful. He is a kind person. Please don't call the police."

George looked up in astonishment as suddenly Fila appeared out from the hallway. She had already visited the bathroom and even straightened her hair out. She looked fresh and radiant. George thought his wife and daughter were pretty, but he had never seen a face so beautiful. He sat frozen.

"Dad. This is Fila. We had a long talk last night. Mom!

Mom! Come in here, quick! Wake up Grace too. Fila, please, sit down here, next to me. Let's explain."

———◦———

The unincorporated town of Basalt, Colorado, population about 4000, is half way up the 40 mile road through the middle of the Roaring Fork Valley reaching from the Colorado River town of Glenwood Springs at a 5000 ft. elevation all the way up to the ski resort of Aspen at 8000 ft. elevation. On up past Aspen the winding road continues up - through the heavily wooded White River National Forest and over the Continental Divide at Independence Pass, an elevation of 13,000 ft.

The population of Glenwood Springs, the largest town in the valley, is roughly 10,000 while Aspen and nearby Carbondale are second at approximately 7,000 each. Just a short time ago, the valley was not always so populous. It is thought some 25,000 years ago humans were present in southwestern Colorado, probably tribes traveling from Asia through the straits of Alaska to this new continent. From around 12,000 B.C. to 1300 A.D., evidence of inhabitants, known as the Mesa Verde "Indian" culture, is widespread over the area of the American Southwest. In 1541 the Spanish explorer Coronado briefly touched the land of the now state of Colorado.

The scene changed dramatically and quickly during the second half of the 19th century as so many discovery events unfolded. In 1859, gold was found in Idaho Springs, a small settlement just west of Denver, the large trading town at the foot of the Rockies. The rush to discover minerals was on, and in 1860 Leadville near the Continental Divide became the second most populous town in what was deemed the Colorado Territory in 1861. A soldier from Indiana named Captain Richard Sopris headed up a group of gold seekers in 1860 to explore farther west. Following the Eagle River from Denver, the company crossed the Continental Divide and came upon the hot springs of what is now Glenwood Springs, turned south up the Roaring Fork Valley, and explored up to an eye-catching, beautiful stand alone twin peaked 13,000 ft. mountain, halfway up the valley. They named it Sopris Peak, now called Mount Sopris. Captain Sopris found no gold but after three months of exploring returned to Denver, and his notes and measurements helped shape the first government map of Colorado.

The Ute Indians, known to have been inhabitants of the area for some 5000 years, did not take the encroachment of the white man searching for minerals lightly. Harsh conflict became unavoidable, started by both sides. The 1864 Massacre at Sand Creek, a Cheyenne and Arapahoe Indian village near Denver, set the stage. Despite the Indians flying U.S. and white flags as indications of a peace, 700 U.S. soldiers indiscriminately murdered inhabitants and even left to the cold helpless women and children. Conflict in the Roaring Fork Valley reached its climax in 1879 with the Meeker Massacre. The Utes attacked Indian Agent Nathan Meeker and his ten male employees, holding their children as hostages. A U.S. Army contingent was called in, and its Major and thirteen of his troops were killed. The conflict led to a forced removal of most of the Utes in Colorado farther west to Utah which then opened millions of acres to white settlement.

———————◆●————————

"Dad, do you understand now?" Zachary's voice trembled. "We have no way to take her back. Our nation is in turmoil. Let's just let her stay with us until things get sorted out. It's the Christian thing to do."

George straightened up, looking intently at Zachary, his

deep voice rising. The sturdy looking man who one would think at first appearance as being authoritative, one who would immediately command respect, barked out. "Son! Christ be damned. Hogwash! We were informed from the news reports she is part of an assassin group from a foreign country. For your beloved Christ's sake, they killed the President of the United States! How can we possibly trust her?"

"George! Stop!" Colleen interjected calmly but forcefully. "Zachary is right. We know she has repented. We know she gained the support of Michael Reynolds. She turned things around for him. We know she is conflicted, but I also know from seeing her for the first time, from looking at her face, hearing her voice, she is not dangerous. It is our Christian duty to help her, not turn her over to the police whose hands are full in this emergency, this crisis. While you have rejected the notion of a loving God, you still believe in our values. You …"

"Okay, okay," a more sullen George sat back. "Stop preaching." While George listened to his wife's defense, he was also staring at Fila, this time much more intently while she and Zachary told the story how she walked two hundred miles over eight nights to arrive on their doorstep cold, hungry and exhausted. Her unique look, her facial appearance, her stunning features, the visual look, but to top all that off was George's second take when Zachary made her rise briefly to help pull her jacket off. George was listening to Colleen's appeal but could not help missing a glance at Fila's bodily shape. The tight jeans, the snug shirt revealing her ample bosom – *my goodness, she's perfect,* he marveled. For George suddenly – a complete turnaround.

The room fell silent, everyone looking down exploring their own thoughts, except for young Grace who continued to stare at Fila in awe. She had never seen such a natural beauty. A minute later, Fila stood up and gently grabbed her coat from the sofa. "I have caused enough trouble here. I will go. I know how to survive in the mountains if you can just get me started with a few supplies. I…"

"No, no way! Winter is coming. I will not let you go," an impassioned Zachary shouted as he rose up next to her.

"Both of you – sit down right now," George countered. "No one is going anywhere. We are fortunate that Colleen here had a huge vegetable and potato garden going this summer. We have food stocked. Lots of water from our river. We escaped the virus. We have a ton of fuel for our emergency generator, lots of firewood for our stove and fireplace. We have shotguns to hunt. We keep our satellite phones powered up to hear news of what's going on the rest of the country, and while it's not good news, we here are lucky -- we stay right here." The strong voice of authority. Zachary pushed down on Fila's arm, and they both sat down. Grace looked down and smiled.

"Thank you, dear. That's the most sensible thing I've heard in a month," Colleen softly responded, looking graciously to George then to Zachary and Fila. A new sense of calm settled in as the five sat in quiet.

Four

"I'm at wits end, Rose. How do we find her? My only guess is she walked to the mountains. I saw her looking at our book of maps. An Afghan girl, mountain people. Survivors. Maybe she thinks she can hid and survive high up in the mountains. But she only took a light jacket. She didn't steal any money or food from us. I have tried to contact the police in towns west of here, but they have their hands full with sick people getting over the virus, those that died, with food shortages, with power outages. They sure haven't seen any Afghan girl." Michael stared ahead.

Across the candlelight dinner table trying to get one year old Alex to eat his dinner of macaroni and cheese, Rose grimaced slightly. "Michael, give it up. You have too many things to do at the university – -still trying how to figure out how we get people well again with the shortage of good water, vitamins and food. How we get all those burned out transformers back on line. The problem of the virus spreading further, thank God, is diminishing quickly, but getting food from our farms distributed, from the boats pouring in from South America, the supply of fuel to the millions of emergency generators running around the country. It's overwhelming. Let her go for now."

What Rose could never fathom is how a man's rational mind

is often undermined by his natural instincts to be attracted emotionally to the appeal of a member of the opposite sex whom he has become close to – a paramount genetic instinct going back hundreds of thousands, maybe millions, of years. Order in the any society requires a strong set of rules and customs. To Michael, the issues Rose raised of course are the most pressing, but in his daily thinking in the month since he first met Fila, he simply could not get thoughts of her out of his mind. Worse, she had lived in their apartment for three weeks -- she was not a casual acquaintance. Yes, she was incredibly attractive physically, but she was also bore this captivating mystique -- her soft voice, her way of thinking offering divergent, complex motives, her internal conflict, her search for answers, for the quest for Truth. No, Michael could not let it go. He harbored the same thoughts – *why this violence?*

⬤

The beauty in western Colorado in autumn is spectacular. In late September early October, daytime temperatures are quite pleasant with typical low humidity, making the afternoons, well, perfect. The strong summer thunderstorms are over. The green pines on the mountains blended with the magnificent yellow and gold leafs of the abundant aspen trees leaves one breathless. But Michael knew the nights get increasingly colder with snow appearing at the higher elevations. This girl, no matter what her upbringing in rugged Afghanistan might have been, had no resources. *She has no money, no blankets, heavy clothing, a place of shelter, no protection from mountain lions – I cannot leave her on her own.* Michael could not get Fila off his mind. He knew she did not want to be identified. She would not be walking into any towns seeking assistance. Maybe she would finally give out, find a stranger who might help her get through the coming winter. By Sunday October 23rd, his patience gave out. A day off from the think tank at the university; the vast solar power array along with the large number of emergency generators there had kept electricity flowing. He could fully charge his Chevy Volt electric vehicle and start driving west, stopping at each town and asking anyone he could find -- any word of a bronze-skinned woman with green eyes walking through the area? *What would be in her mind? What was her most logical route? She came to us from the West. She would go back that way.*

Michael figured that from their apartment atop the former Four Seasons she could walk a few blocks south and pick up 6th Avenue, which is also Route 6, the oldest transcontinental highway going from Provincetown, Massachusetts to Long Beach, California. Going west she would soon come to Golden, then follow route 6 into the rural areas to the first mountain town of Idaho Springs, some 30 miles from Denver. She would have plenty of water along the way as the route paralleled the Clear Creek then the Eagle River. Not wanting to be discovered, perhaps she might walk only at night in the dark, maybe 25 miles per night by the light of the stars. She probably wouldn't know that Route 6 also at times becomes the same road as the much newer Interstate 70, but in the midst of the nation's electrical crisis there would be very few vehicles on the road at night. The big hurdle would be the Continental Divide, another 30 miles away. The Eisenhower tunnel through the Divide is a mile and a half in length. *She wouldn't risk that walk for fear of being discovered - nowhere to hide.* Before the tunnel, Route 6 breaks off and makes a long steep, narrow, curving way up and over at the Loveland Pass - an arduous hike but quite navigable.

Then I-70 picks up again down at the valley and the town of Frisco, 20 miles from the Loveland peak. Lots of gradually sloped bike paths then appear and make the 25 mile journey pass Copper Mountain and up over the Vail Pass not too difficult. She would now discover a long valley and find it easy to hide along Route 6 again. After experiencing some cold nights, *would she try to settle here somewhere for the winter?* If she kept going another 30 miles along the valley, she would then have to navigate the incredible 15 miles of the Glenwood Canyon ending up at the town of Glenwood Springs. One of the most beautiful, scenic canyons anywhere, deep and very narrow with a roaring river in the middle and twisting tight railroad tracks on one side and curvy I-70 on the other. If she took that route she could very easily be confused and worn out at the canyon's end. *Maybe at Glenwood Springs, the bottom of the Roaring Fork Valley, hungry and tired, she might call it quits.*

"Michael! For heaven's sake!" Rose's voice rose to a fever pitch. "Sunday is your day with us. You need to relax a little. You have been driving yourself every day at the university. You can't just go off searching for her. We have what we need to know about her associates and where she came from and why they attacked us. Leave it alone! Let it rest!

"And what's more, let me add, President Graham has received some limited communications from the Chinese government that those responsible for the 9/11 attacks have been held accountable. There will be no more. It's done."

Car keys in his hand, a determined Michael looked down as he spoke slowly and calmly. "No, I'm sorry. I'm sorry. It's not done, Rose. We do not fully understand their methods and their motives. And how did they obtain a powerful atom bomb, and how did they launch it so perfectly? With weapons of mass destruction like this, so available to not just a rogue nation but to a terrorist few, these strikes can happen again and again. We have to figure all this out…. Honey, certainly I want to help our country pull out of this crisis, but we also have to stop this from happening again. The first 9/11 was certainly devastating but this 9/11, hundreds of times worse. Can we afford another? I'm just going to Golden and Idaho Springs. I can be back in two hours. Trust me."

———— • ————

"No, no I haven't seen any such person passing through." Michael thanked each person he quizzed out on the streets of Golden and then uphill and upstream to the mountain town of Idaho Springs. He stopped in gas stations, only a couple which were open, and any open store selling food to ask the same question. "An attractive young woman, dark complexion, dark hair, striking green eyes, walking alone west. See her?" Two hours driving that first Sunday and then back to Rose and Alex. Each Sunday thereafter, an extra hour, and extra town, until pay dirt. Six hours round trip -- Glenwood Springs.

Five

"Okay. Now here's how we settle this until all this craziness gets sorted out. We will have to trust you, Fila, but you have to be open and visible with us. Grace has twin beds in her room. You will sleep in there. I have some night garments and other clothes that may fit you. You will have to earn your keep. We have to conserve our emergency generator fuel and firewood. Well, we can always get more of that when we need it, but we heat the house only first thing in the morning and before dinner. You will help me with the garden, fetching water, and with the cooking." Colleen was on a roll. She had taken charge. George, Zachary, Fila and Grace sat with faces aghast. Full attention.

Colleen continued calmly, straightforward. "I work three days a week at St. Vincent Catholic Church. It's about a mile walk from here. Right on Midland Avenue in the heart of Basalt. You will go with me. We need more help in this emergency. There are folks short on food and power." Then softly, "The Lord's prayers are going to be answered." And she added strongly, "Let's see … it's Monday, October 11. We go tomorrow morning, nine o'clock."

Raised in Indiana within a strongly religious family, Colleen attended the nearby University of Notre Dame majoring in religious studies but dropped out after two years to attend to her mother who was suffering a long and eventually terminal cancer illness. While attending a cancer care center to gather nursing information, she met a strong looking, very handsome young man who was there for the same reason – George Gelayes. His dad was also suffering from a terminal cancer condition. George had a deep, powerful voice and sounded very authoritative, but he was extremely polite. He recited how his dad had worked very hard in the US Steel mill in Gary, Indiana and had wanted his son to attend college and obtain a less bodily-stressed administrative job. George acquiesced and attended Valparaiso University in Indiana majoring in business administration, but never liked his first two desk jobs out of college. He developed an urge to move to rugged Colorado and enjoy the outdoor life. At the same time he felt a sense of futility in believing in an all-loving god when his father and the mother of newly met, beautiful Colleen, could die agonizing deaths from cancer, both only in their late 40's.

What was initially empathy for each other's family situations grew into a strong bond of love between the two, dating each weekend, marrying within a year's time. Their physical and mental attraction for each other overcame Colleen's initial negative reaction to his suggested move to Colorado. But more importantly, the pair somehow quietly put aside their major religious differences – he now an outright atheist and she a devoted Catholic worshiper. Their mutually strong moral values of work, family, and community overcame any differences about who or what guides their daily actions or what happens after they die. That conflicting interplay certainly influenced their son Zachary's decision to learn as much as he could when attending college about the different major religions of the world. *How do my parents get along so well with such divergent views about their very existence? Why doesn't the world get along like they do?*

That rest of that day and evening, Fila faithfully followed Colleen's every move, every suggestion, every directive. She remained quiet, submissive, thankful for these generous Americans, just like Michael and Rose, being so kind to her. Other than that mad scientist, Jonathan Dean, every American she had met seemed the opposite of what was painted to her during her mission training on Dire. Americans were not monsters intent on initiating acts of violence. *How could Aazim and Antoine have been so wrong?* The thought now haunted her more and more. While there was little conversation the rest of that day, George and Zachary could not resist taking a sneak glance at Fila every chance they could. She didn't have the opportunity to notice their stares as Colleen kept her so busy.

At breakfast the next morning, words were polite but few. "Good morning." "How did you sleep?" "How is your breakfast?" "More coffee?" Colleen's smooth tone of voice moved it on. "Okay gang. George, more firewood. Zach, please clean up the front and back porches. Gracie, you're coming with us. Fila, get your hat and jacket. We're walking to town." Colleen -- the new authority.

The Gelayes home sat near the start of Two Rivers Road just off the main Roaring Fork Valley road of Route 82. A slightly elevated position but not much of any big view across the highway below or behind where a steep mountain base stood fairly close. Comfortable, spacious, not deluxe, not poor. It had privacy as the first road up from Two Rivers Road soon branched into cul-de-sac Silverado Road to the right with five nice homes and Hillcrest Drive to the left, a road that snaked up the mountainside a ways with homes on both sides. However, the Gelayes home was at the dead end of a short branch off Hillcrest just as it began its first turn upwards. Therefore, a quite private setting and the initial attraction for Fila. As the main road Highway 82 crossed the Roaring Fork River at that intersection of Two Rivers Road and continued on to the right headed towards Aspen, the narrow Two Rivers Road followed the river path on its left up to the downtown of Basalt, about a mile.

"So here we are, 'bout in the middle of civilization in this valley. You must have come through Glenwood Springs, the big hot springs everybody loves. Big attraction. That's twenty miles that way down valley, only 'bout five thousand foot altitude there; here we are almost seven thousand foot elevation, and another twenty miles up valley is the famous ski town of Aspen, bout eight thousand feet high. After that it's all forest and very beautiful all the way up to Independence Pass, 'bout thirteen thousand." Fila nodded her head and listened intently to Colleen's geography lesson as the three started their walk to town. Grace strode along gingerly, right up close to Fila's side.

"So let me tell you about our little town coming up here. This big mass you see on the left, Fila, is Basalt Mountain, first called Black Mountain. Named that way because under the tree foliage it's a dark rock from lava flows, low in silica and high in iron. I'm told basalt is the most common rock on the surface of the earth and on the ocean floors. It's the dark areas you see on the moon. Can't see much here, but when we get into town you'll see better how massive the mountain is. And I think almost eleven thousand feet high at the summit.... Now, the town. It's at the meeting of two rivers, the Roaring Fork coming down south from Aspen and the Frying Pan from the east. They call it the confluence here, the coming together of two rivers.

When minerals and silver were first discovered out here, the little settlement was called Frying Pan Town, that name from the abundant trout caught upstream here that supposedly were cooked in frying pans. You will see the remains of kilns just above downtown. They were used to produce charcoal from wood used as a fuel for the miners flocking to Aspen, where silver was discovered, I think about eighteen eighty. The heat of the kilns drives moisture out of the wood, making it less smoky when burning. It also burns at a higher temperature than wood and makes it much more fuel efficient. Later on, coal was discovered in Carbondale, a town bout ten miles west from here, and so the kilns shut down. Funny, the town's name didn't come from coal discovered there, but because the original settlers came from Carbondale, Pennsylvania.

"Well, what started as a small settlement took off when the railroads finally arrived here. I think it was eighteen eighty two …"

"No, Mom," Grace piped in. "It was silver in Aspen in eighteen eighty-two but no big deal here until the railroad arrived here, and that was in eighteen eighty seven."

"Okay, you're right, dear. Paying attention in school, huh? So two railroads were racing here from different directions during that new Silver Rush. The Rio Grande was building tracks up the valley from Glenwood Springs and the competing Colorado Midland Railroad over the mountains from Leadville. Now this is really interesting. Leadville was already a big mining town, but up the Frying Pan River; it was over the Continental Divide, not far in miles but what a huge engineering task to extend their tracks to here. The labor, and the human toil, gigantic. They actually built curving, winding wooden platforms for the tracks high up from Leadville on that side, then down on this side towards here. Our name was changed to Aspen Junction when the two train companies met here, and maintenance sheds were constructed here – we became a rail yard."

"And which railroad got to Aspen first?" Fila was enraptured with the tale.

"Okay, but let me finish first. No one talks about it now, but a lot of those hardworking railroad people were imported from China. It was hard work in tough conditions, and a lot of them suffered, some died. Up and down wooden trestles in snow in the winter, but first they had to drill through the Continental Divide, almost twelve thousand feet there. They drilled a tunnel, the Hagerman Tunnel, a couple thousand feet through, just five hundred feet below the summit, you say in eighteen eighty seven, Grace. But anyhow, the Rio Grande got here first and on to Aspen first."

"So interesting, Colleen, please go on. But first, I just glanced that way and I have a view of that mountain over there. What is that?" Fila queried.

"Oh, right. That is our gem. We hike up to the top in summer. That's about the only one or two stand-alone mountains in Colorado. We have over 30 fourteen thousand foot peaks, but they are all part of ranges. That beauty there stands alone. It's twin peaked, which you see perfectly from here…. That's Mount Sopris."

"Beautiful," sighed Fila. Grace smiled broadly.

"Well the booming population here and around Aspen ended quickly when the United States went off the silver standard in eighteen ninety three and prices dropped real fast. Just as sudden, the population in Aspen and Basalt dropped significantly, and as they say in America 'boom to bust'. That's when we changed the town's name here to Basalt… yup, from an Indian Reservation to Frying Pan Town to Aspen Junction to Basalt. And very little activity came back here until skiing in Aspen became the next boom in the nineteen sixties. And then came us, George and Colleen, to enjoy the outdoor life."

"Indian Reservation? What was that?"

"A whole another story, a whole 'nother story. You'll learn, Fila, you'll learn. Nothing in this life comes easy. The Lord works it all His way."

———————————•◦•———————————

"We're almost there, Mom," Grace spoke up hurriedly. "Isn't this going to be a little complicated? I thought Fila is hiding, I mean I thought Fila is trying not to be identified who she really is." The three fell silent for a moment. All looked down, somber, as they walked with the buildings of downtown Basalt now in view. The town really has just two parallel commercial streets, each only a hundred yards long, with a short street headed back to Route 82 with a modern library and post office on it. Saint Vincent Catholic Church is a modest structure at the end of the commercial buildings on the main street, Midland Avenue. The two mountain rivers meet and into one, the confluence, just below the middle of town, close to Route 82. Above the main streets towards the path of the Frying Pan River, one finds schools and well-groomed residential areas. Probably even some nice winter homes for the Aspen skiers.

"Okay, right, this is the story," Colleen brightened. "Fila, you are going to meet Father Richard Jensen, our Pastor. Your name is biblical, you're Mary, Mary Matthews. You're from the Caribbean Islands, Dominican Republic, olive skin, green eyes, a real mix, but your family brought you here as a young child, to New York. You don't even remember how to speak Spanish. You're what almost thirty years old?"

"Thirty three. I'm thirty three."

"Well, whatever, you look good," Colleen was quick to

respond, "even after your walking ordeal." Colleen shrugged, looking not quite sure what to say after that. Grace smiled. Fila looked down, expressionless.

Only a few people were on the streets as they passed the darkened stores. They looked closed. No electricity, no customers. Only shops that had candles in stock had seen any business the last month. The few number of restaurants had quickly run out of food supplies – mainly taken home by owners and employees. At least the virus had not found its way here.

The Basalt area's electric power began in 1885 with the building of a commercially operated hydroelectric plant, mainly to supply current to the booming silver town of Aspen. Not much electricity growth followed until the renewed spurt of population in the valley in the mid to late 20th century. The Holy Cross Energy Co-op, headquartered in Glenwood Springs, grew proportionally with over 50,000 users by 2015, with energy supplied by long-term contracts with the Public Service Company of Colorado and the Western Area Power Administration. The problem at 9/11/2021 was that their sources of generation were over 60% from coal and gas, and those power lines were not now transmitting any high voltage current. Transformers spread along the distribution lines which reduce and control electrical voltages had been massively burned out from the huge surge sent to earth from the electromagnetic pulse set off by the nuclear explosion high above Kansas. The Co-op could give no timetable when its power supply would be restored.

"Father, this is our friend, Mary Matthews. She's staying with us a while. She lives alone down the valley, and we have agreed we would all do better getting through this situation if we helped each other out. She has also agreed to help us here."

"Well, good, Colleen…. Nice to meet you, Mary," Father

Jensen offered, greeting Fila kindly and putting out his hand warmly. A pleasant face, receding gray hair nicely combed back, ruddy complexion, a man of some 70 years of age, Fila guessed. *Another kind American* - Fila's first impression.

"And where are you from, Mary, originally I mean?" Father Jensen quizzed. "I must say, you have a very distinct look, I mean, I say that kindly, not looking like the typical folks we see in the valley. I mean...." An awkward moment ensued. Fila stared blankly ahead.

Colleen immediately stepped in, not giving Fila a chance to play with an answer. "Father, she is quite shy. She was actually born in Santo Domingo, Dominican Republic ... you can see of mixed heritage, but grew up in New York."

"Oh, Catholic then," he replied with a beaming smile.

Again, Colleen took the lead as Fila's face showed confusion. The last thing the two of them wanted to admit to this American priest was that she was raised a Muslim in Afghanistan. Too complicated. "Father, she doesn't like to talk about it. You know, New York City, secular with the young these days and yet full of all the religions of the world with that diverse population there."

"Right, right. Well what I wanted to tell you this morning, Colleen, is that members of our Chamber of Commerce used our hall last night to talk about getting our kilns up the hill there to operate again. They are in pretty good shape – you know, they really have been a tourist attraction for the last hundred years. We sure have lots of wood in these parts, and not knowing when we get our electrical power back, it sure would be a good idea to prepare for winter by having charcoal for our stoves and fireplaces.... Do you think George could be interested in helping out?"

"Father, yes, for sure, and Zach too. I'll tell them today. Great idea. We have to get ready for winter."

Father Jensen's kind face showed a smile, and then turned to a frown. "Right, we'll survive the cold, but you and I, Colleen - you are the brightest, most hard working volunteer I have helping this parish. If this situation goes on for long, you know ... it's food. Food shortages. Very few trucks are getting to Glenwood on the interstate. Every market in the valley now is about bare. I fear..."

"I know, Father, I know. We have so many out there without the resources. Let's sit down and talk."

———•———

That evening back home, the conversation continued. "Look, I got it, Colleen! Stop beating on it ... you and your priest are right. Food for our community is going to be all-important if this electricity doesn't get back on soon. Electric vehicles can't get enough power and gasoline pumps can't be pumped without current." George paused, looking down. "So the food markets ... I know, they are running low. Not everyone has an emergency generator with enough of a fuel source. Just lucky we have a tank full of diesel, and I have rigged a hand pump to get it to the generator. and we have the solar. At least we can keep some lights and our refrigerator running." The dinner table fell quiet among the five. Colleen had made her point about food quite clear and about her many fellow church parishioners and town folks who were without electricity all together, and those who did not have gardens, and those who did not have rifles to hunt game or fishing rods and bait to catch trout.

"Dad, aren't there lots of potato farms in the valley? I ..." Zachary restarted the conversation.

"No, no, son," George interrupted. "That was back in the silver mining days, to feed the miners. Long gone."

As Colleen rose to clear dishes from the table, she looked at

George. "Wait, isn't there such a thing as winter wheat? Planted in the Fall and it's ready in early Spring. George?"

"Hmmm, that's a thought. Let's find out…. Okay, tomorrow, when I follow up with the Chamber of Commerce guys about the idea of getting those old kilns going, I'll also make sure our hunting licenses get suspended and go past the usual end of September to end of November dates, and okay dear I'll also find out bout winter wheat. That may be a great idea if this crazy situation goes on for long. Course we might still have to find ways to grind it into flour, like the old days."

Fila finally entered the conversation, not hesitant about her accent. "Yes, growing up in Afghanistan, my family, we all helped out turning wheat into flour and into our bread, and like you now, we went to the streams for our water."

George and Zachary, sitting perfectly still, looked wide-eyed at Fila injecting herself into the conversation, while Colleen and Grace, clearing dishes to the sink, both broke into wide smiles.

Grace joined in. "Okay, so before all this, how did all our markets here get their food supplies?"

"Most of it - big food service companies in big trucks from Denver supplying all the way along I-70," Colleen jumped in. Fila gazed all around the table gaining all this new knowledge about life in the Roaring Creek Valley.

"Fine," George interjected, "but what you're going to find is that from an early mostly agricultural society to an industrial, commercial society the number of farms today is about one third what they were a hundred years ago, and that the great plains of Iowa and Nebraska next to us produce vast quantities of corn and wheat that I bet will be in high demand right now to the East and west to Denver, shutting us out. No, and you'll learn there won't be any free federal land given out for farming like back in 1862's Homestead Act where the government encouraged the growth of the West by giving 160 acres free land to hundreds of thousands of settler families. And Zach, our big flat eastern Colorado is not so rich in soil and is mostly small family farms…. And all those ranches west and south of us will be holding on to their cattle for beef to themselves. No, guys, we 're gonna have to fend for ourselves."

And George added: "Yeah, and even though the last dozen years we've had some pick up in local farming, it's not enough. Pitkin County here has had a program for young farming entrepreneurs to lease land and cultivate, I think lettuce, beets, carrots onions, garlic, squash, mushrooms, fruit trees, you name it, but I'm sure your Father Jensen knows they sure did not produce enough to supply every one here over the winter."

"Yes, Father Jensen does know that," Colleen added. "And he knows the few farms here that raise chickens and lambs to sell to the Farmers' Markets don't have nearly enough production. He is also aware the great little town back through the mountains, Paonia, settled years ago by farmers and ranchers now famous for its fruit orchards, simply can't have that much a supply left."

While all looked down and somber at those remarks, Grace suddenly piped up: "Dad! How did you get so smart?" George broke into a little smile, and looked at Fila's wide eyes for approving recognition, but Fila quickly dropped her glances at both Grace and George.

Zachary squirmed in his chair as he finished up his fish, potatoes, and spinach dinner. "Still cannot connect to any search engine sites on my laptop or cell phone, but darn it, I'm going to the library tomorrow and research farming and ranching out in this part of the country. There has to be a food supply."

———————⬥•⬤———————

As dusk turned to darkness that third evening of Fila's presence, candles were moved to the living room and the five spread out in the comfortable seating there. Colleen was the first to speak up. "Fila, we Americans are so used to watching television after dinner but with no programming on, we have been playing this card game – pinochle. We can teach it to you if …"

Six

A cross the candlelight dinner table Rose grimaced while trying to get one year old Alex to eat his dinner of macaroni and cheese. Agitated, she spoke up. "Com' on, Michael, give it up. You have too many things to do at the university – we still have to keep trying to figure out how we get people well again with the shortage of good water, vitamins and food. How do we get all those burned out transformers back on line. Thank God the problem of the virus spreading further is diminishing quickly, but getting food from our farms distributed, from the boats pouring in from South America, the supply of fuel to the millions of emergency generators running around the country. It's overwhelming. Let her go for now."

But the next day was Sunday. He could not let her go.

By early November, Michael had covered all the towns spreading west from Denver along the combination of Route 6 and I-70. Golden, Idaho Springs, Georgetown, Silverton, Frisco, Copper, Vail, Avon, Eagle – everyone he asked, no sighting of a unique young woman walking alone. On Sunday, November 7, Michael ventured past the pastures and rolling hills that graced the land before Glenwood Canyon and continued down the 15 miles of winding highway surrounded by its majestic canyon walls and along side its roaring river. It was his first trip here into this long, narrow canyon. He was so mesmerized by its incredible views that he almost forgot his mission. Then quite suddenly, the end of the canyon appeared and there was the town of Glenwood Springs.

It was a clear, blue-sky day, and a brisk 50 degrees at noon after a 23 degree early morning start. After parking his 200 mile range Chevy Volt at a gas station offering electric charging from its propane powered electric generator, Michael walked back down the main street asking the same question of everyone who would stop and listen. Dejected after all the "no, I haven't" responses, he dragged himself back to his electric vehicle for the 170 mile drive back to Denver. *Maybe I was just wrong, her heading west. Maybe she is just up in the hills outside Denver. Maybe she went south towards Colorado Springs.* The gas station attendant by his car was a different person than when he had arrived.

Looking quite solemn, Michael asked this one last person as he reached into his pocket for his roll of cash. " It's been a two hour charge. Should do it. How much do I owe you? … and oh, by the way, were you here, back around the start of the month?"

"Yeah, my dad owns this station. The only way we're making a living so we can buy the little bit of food that arrives here in town is to keep this generator running. We've been lucky to have a good source of propane gas to run it. I'm here every afternoon and early evening…. Why? What's up?"

Michael took a deep breath and thought *okay, one last try.* "I'm looking for a friend who became confused and lost from the 9/11 attack. She wandered off, and we think she walks alone after dark. She is in her early 30's, very attractive, medium build, olive skin, green eyes. Any chance you've seen her passing through?" Michael looked down, waiting for the usual answer.

But after a long silence, he looked up again at the young man, who was staring out towards the highway, his brow furrowed.

"Yeah, yeah, I sure have," he finally replied. "So that's it, huh. Yeah, she sure looked traumatized. Lost, huh?" He paused.

Michael's eyes abruptly opened wide, pleading for more. "Go on, then you did see her. Where was she going? Was she walking alone? Did you talk to her?"

"Look, it was wild. It was near dark. I was about to close up. She had an accent. She had an empty water bottle in her hand. She saw our water fountain over there by the door. She asked me if she could fill her bottle up. I said 'sure'. Then I got a good look at her close up. She, she…."

"Go on, she what? Go on, she what?"

"You said she was attractive, but boy I've never seen someone that beautiful. I tried to strike up a conversation, but she wouldn't respond. I offered to help her. She was alone, walked up to this station by herself. I offered to escort her home. She just walked up to the water jug and filled up her bottle. I kept asking her questions, and she just looked at me with the inside light now on her face. I couldn't figure her out. She looked so good, but very tired, slow moving. I felt helpless…."

"Okay, and then, what did she do?" Michael's attention heightened. He could feel his heart pounding.

"She just put the cap back on her bottle, looked at me with a smile, and said 'Thank you. You are very kind…. Am I right -- this is the road up to Independence?'

And then she started to walk off into the dark. I said 'Yes, but it's fifty miles, you can't' … I heard a faint 'thank you' but then she was just gone…. So tell me, who was she?"

"Okay, thanks," Michael followed on excitedly. "She is a good friend of my family. She is a foreign student staying with us in Denver while going to graduate school. Like I said, she just couldn't get over the 9/11 attack from foreigners, so she just took off, confused. I have to get back to Denver now, but I'll be back later to look for her.... Listen, in case you hear anything more about her, call my satellite cell phone. It works all the time. Here's my name and number." Looking bewildered, John Striver nodded, still holding Michael's cash as Michael hurriedly entered his recharged Volt and speedily took off back towards I-70.

"John. I'm John Striver," the astonished attendant said to no one.

Seven

Life under duress became routine in Basalt. Winter was coming fast in mid-November with regular snowfalls appearing on the mountain tops, especially on Mt. Sopris. Those persons able bodied enough who could hunt and fish did so. Everyone involved seemed to have ample ammunition and fishing rods. With Colleen's and Fila' assistance in gaining community support, all who shot game and caught fish donated 25% of their bounty to Father Jensen's Catholic Church, who in turn distributed it to his needy parishioners and to welcoming non-parishioners alike. Members of the Chamber of Commerce, along with the assistance of the able bodied like George and Zachary, were able to restore working order to three of the old brick kilns, supply them with firewood, heat and convert the wood to moisture free charcoal, and distribute the gain to town residents. Backbreaking work but doable.

Only now in late November was Fila beginning to feel more and more comfortable in her role as a family helper. She figured with the ongoing electricity crisis in America, no one was going to come looking for her, especially in the winter. Even so, she could not relinquish nightly those grim thoughts of her coming to America as an assassin, of Michael Reynolds' and Rose Haines's remarkable kindness shown her, of Michael's insatiable curiosity of herself -- pressing to find answers to all the questions of understanding life and death, kindness and violence. Each night after saying good night to the darling, ever-inquisitive Grace, she found sleep impossible for at least an hour.

Even after saying 'good night' to Grace and Grace then hopping out of her twin bed to reach over and plant a kiss on Fila's cheek, Fila would not slumber off until silently reciting the same questions to herself about good and evil, peace and violence. Now the added questions each night. *I can understand Zachary's constant questioning – he wants to know just like I do what's going on in this life, and if there is a next. He's highly intelligent. Can he help me understand? Colleen is so straightforward, so unbroken in her faith. Could anyone evil ever undo that strong moral ground? But George, so strong a man but he makes me uncomfortable with his stares. When Colleen is not there, he tells me how pretty I am and how nice it is to have me with his family. But can I trust him if we are ever alone? I have seen those looks from men before; I know what they are after.* And finally, sleep.

For the five of the Gelayes household, the days were physically arduous, and after dinner bed rest was the calling. Only young Grace had a break in the hard work when her schoolteacher called her students offering two-hour teaching sessions at the town's modern library. The structure featured one solid glass side from the floor all the way up to a high ceiling. While the design was a feature of clearly seeing the lower side of nearby Basalt mountain, it was perfect for allowing enough natural light in for the students to read and converse. Fila was becoming more relaxed in this setting and gradually getting use to being called 'Mary, Mary Matthews,' by the town and church folk. But she tried her best not to return the glances of the young men who seemed to stare at her too long or too hard. The last thing she wanted in her life was a new romance.

For the past two months, George had only been thinking about his own family's well-being – shotguns and ample ammunition to hunt game just a short hike away, up into the vast wilderness area of the White River National Forest which surrounded both sides of the valley. Lots of elk and mule deer roaming both sides, bighorn sheep above the Frying Pan River, and even black bear by Mt. Sopris. And then there was Colleen's large garden with ample vegetables and potatoes.

Around 8 each morning, bathrobe clad Colleen had the coffee ready to pour before George usually wandered into the kitchen in jeans, a T shirt and bare feet. As usual the wood-burning stove had already taken the chill out of the air. Then for George and often Zachary, it was bundling up, gathering their guns and ammunition, and off for the mountains to hunt. The girls cleaned up the kitchen, straightened the beds, then out to fetch nearby river water in their pails, carry it back home and boil it on the kitchen stove in case it contained the sickening Giardia parasite common to Colorado streams. In addition to fireplaces, it seemed every household had at least one metal stove. The Gelayes were not alone in their water chores. As the municipal water company could rarely get their pumps working, buckets of water taken from the flowing rivers were filled every morning and carried home by the town's women and girls.

Every Friday, a large electrically powered truck would fill up its cargo bay with cans of fruit and vegetables in Glenwood Springs and make an all day journey up the valley stopping in each population center like Jebel, Carbondale, Basalt, Snowmass, and Aspen. There was a simple $1 charge for each can a resident purchased, with a limit of 4 cans per family member per week. The federal government had established the distribution program utilizing existing United States stocks plus the cans of food pouring in from Canada, Mexico, and South America. Local supplies of fresh fruit and vegetables had long been consumed, and food imports of anything fresh were being consumed by residents living closest to their ports of entry.

The male and female duties were each quite different at the Gelayes residence. Fila seemed quite happy to speedily help Colleen clear the dinner table and head off to Grace's bedroom for the night. Grace would quickly follow, for the many questions she had about boys and sex were difficult to discuss with her very religious Catholic mother. At 14, she was already showing a full figure, which for sure was catching the attention of her boy classmates. Fila enjoyed forging this female relationship. All her time with Colleen was rewarding, but it was stern – for Colleen, we work hard to care for our family and to help those in need. It was God's calling, our duty, the centerpiece of our morality. For Grace, it was discovering who she was, her place in life, the extent of her relationships, the balancing of her unleashed womanhood hormones and emotions with the reasonable expectations of restraint placed upon her by her parents, church and school. It seemed to Grace that she must have asked Fila a million questions, and Fila answered them all with understanding, warmth, and clarity.

"Fine Grace, the boys are aggressive as you say. So you kiss a boy you really like, but know his male hormones are then really racing, and he wants to go further. He desires more. You allow that only as a strong bond of a relationship develops, one of mutual respect. You don't go all the way even with protection of contraceptives. You take responsibility, be the one in control.

You wait until marriage, as the last thing you or the boy wants is a child not ready yet to be born into this world."

With each conversation, Fila drew from her own experience. Becoming a young teenager when the Taliban was in charge and all the stories of their sex slaves; her escaping that fate when the Americans arrived to Afghanistan in 2003 hunting down al-Qaeda and chasing away the Taliban from national power, back to their remote villages and towns. She discovered she could mature into womanhood in a new Muslim society where women had educational and job opportunities and could earn the respect of men. She had appreciated the traditions of Islam where women were to dress with modesty to avoid harassment from men, but the radicals had carried it all too far. With the desertion by the Americans ten years later, the harsh treatment of women returned, then luckily her escape to the island of Dire. There she found peace but remained confused as to her proper role and relationship with men - until Asa came along. He treated her with a great deal of equality and respect, and she came to love him dearly. Now again, in America, she really did not know what to think, what to believe in, but she could not let young Grace know that. She had to portray a strong moral compass – show her how her physical growth brings out the needs, the differences, and the similarities of male and female.

The new routine was to change into the pajamas Colleen passed to her that second evening, go to the bathroom, brush her teeth with the toothbrush and toothpaste Grace gave her, rinse her face with water from the large jug Zachary had placed in the bathroom, and then apply the facial moisturizer that Grace said she was welcome to use. Trying to go to sleep in the twin bed next to Grace's, Fila's mind would not calm down despite her bodily tiredness. Thinking, questioning.

Madness. Why are people so kind one moment and violent

at another? Are they only kind to each other in times of distress?
These Americans here are all helping each other. They seem kind,
and kind to me. But they have been in many wars. I have read
about the violence in their inner cities. And then there was the
evil American Jonathan Dean. Are we all naturally violent, or
are we by nature also compassionate? Can we be both? My Asa
was so kind to me. We were in love. Then he would become an
assassin. And me – I was raised with violence all around me;
thought I had found peace in Dire. And then, I learned to be a
killer too, or was I trained, brainwashed? I hit Michael Rose on
the back of his head with my rifle, I shot a Marine in the legs. I
was about to assassinate my target. I pointed the gun at her, my
target – I couldn't shoot her with that baby in her arms. What am
I? Who am I? Do we go back and forth, violent - compassionate,
depending upon circumstances? And all our nations, all our
countries, are the same – peaceful one moment and then corrupt
and violent the next. Does God direct us? Or just smile at us, or
frown at us? Free will? Why? And the United Nations – what good
was it, other than provide food relief to refugees? The so -called
Peace Plan of Antoine and Aazim, once so noble, turned out so
utterly gruesome. And they lied and never gave us the vaccine
they claimed. What has become of them ... and all those peace-
loving friends I admired on Dire who had no idea of this horrible
attack on America? The whole world, it is a mess.... Can I find
answers?

Back in Denver at the National University, Michael worked
feverishly in consort with his academic colleagues and with
President Graham back in Washington to figure out how
to solve the most overriding problem the nation of over 300
million people faced – food distribution. For thousands of years

people survived and nations grew with no electricity, but nearby food and water always a must, and they hunted for it or grew it. In days of smaller populations, people would often move to what they called "greener pastures", but now the world's cities -- huge in population while the number of people living on farms greatly diminished.

It would be months before airplanes and railroads were sufficiently functional with the electric currents they needed for guiding planes and switching/signaling for railroad tracks. Trucks – that was the answer. They could get anywhere as long as they had fuel. Some were powered with the newer, more powerful batteries that had been recently invented while most ran on diesel fuel.

Still, Michael could not get Fila off his mind, nor how the weapons the terrorists used were obtained and engineered. He now had a lead to finding Fila. John Striver in Glenwood Springs believes he saw her. Perfect description. To Glenwood Springs 170 miles. His Volt had a range of 200 miles. He was lucky John Striver's gas station had an emergency generator working to recharge his car's battery so that Michael could make it back to Denver. Another 20 miles to the first significant town, Basalt. Another 20 miles to Aspen. Another 10 miles to Independence Pass. *Could she possibly go there? In the winter? She had asked the attendant to confirm its direction. Independence was just a small tent settlement for miners before Aspen developed. A perfect hideout for her, but those miners could hunt and fish and build fires to survive. She can't do that.* So Michael figured 230 miles to Independence, 460 miles round trip – almost two and a half times his Volt's range. There are no longer-life battery cars available to him. So what if this attendant's fuel to charge his generator has run out? What if no other stations in that valley can provide him power? The round trip time even without finding Fila would probably take over 8 hours. And it's already snowing up there, and with this crisis it's doubtful if the plow trucks up there would be running as usual.

Winter was coming fast. The deadly virus was just that – devastating. While it lost its virulence in just a few short weeks and then disappeared, its early toll had been overwhelming. While 90 million Americans were beyond reach of its spread, like those in the Roaring Fork Valley, the virus was responsible for 10 million deaths in just its first week, another 10 million subsequently for a total death toll of 6% of the U.S. population, far surpassing the 1% mortality rate of the infamous 1918 influenza pandemic.

With food supplies pouring into border entrances and seaports during October and November, President Alexis Graham, now back in Washington D.C., faced the mind-boggling task of her government plotting distribution at a time when pumps utilizing electricity sent domestic water through underground pipes, and electric powered pumps pulling up fuel from underground tanks at automotive and truck filling stations were still mainly powerless. The national electric grid was far from back to reasonable order – replacement of burned out transformers the main bottleneck. Michael Reynolds, now the president of the #1 National University in Denver, was busy every waking minute. He learned that while the nation had nearly 20 million portable generators in use, nearly all were designed for limited duration, for brief emergencies. They would need constant repair if overused or used continuously, and secondly most ran on utility company gas, diesel fuel or propane gas, all of which faced supply problems.

Tormented, Michael had to set his mind on doing the best he could on helping to solve the overwhelming problems of the nation. The thoughts of Fila were reserved for the hour it took him to fall asleep each night. Michael's unrelenting thoughts before falling asleep each night exhausted -- *Fila. my mind won't settle down. I have to find you. I must.*

———————•——————

While the abrupt global warming crisis of 2012 through 2018 impacted North America especially hard, the 9/11 attack of 2021, directed primarily to the geography of the United States, was incredibly disastrous. Elsewhere, the non-nuclear pulse bomb explosions, which occurred over many capital cities around the world, were intended to blackmail those nations into giving up their major arms. Any detrimental electromagnetic pulse effects caused limited and temporary damage. They were just not powerful enough. The demented master plan of Antoine and Aazim to bring everlasting peace to the world failed. And as we know, a Chinese nuclear submarine equipped with nuclear missiles ended the dreams of peace for the residents of the island of Dire.

While the majority of electrical generators were still powered by petroleum based diesel fuel, in recent years there had been a tremendous increase in the production of the much cleaner burning biodiesels, the United States utilizing soybean oil as its source. As Michael researched, he found the inventory supply stores of soybean oil were fortunately very high on 9/11/2021. By early November, following a detailed recommendation by Michael, a coalition of cooperating trucking companies was forged under a Presidential and Congressional National Emergency Order. The mandate would coordinate deliveries of petroleum based imports from refineries in Mexico and Brazil as well as biodiesels stocks from U.S. inventories, meet with thousands of trucks at food storage and distribution centers, supply the nation's supermarkets, and promise fair compensation when the crisis was ended. The plan worked. Panic and starvation were avoided. The nation survived the winter of 2022.

In Basalt, where water, fish. game, firewood, and charcoal were plentiful, there too the population survived the winter, obviously much better off than in the larger population centers. In the early Spring of 2022, everyone in the Roaring Fork Valley who had any land planted vegetable and potato seeds and bulbs. Everyone in the Gelayes household stuck to their duties. George and Zachary hunted and fished hours on end. Colleen, Fila and Grace made daily trips to the nearby river and brought back buckets of water to be heated and then distributed around the home in pitchers. They walked to the Catholic Church a mile away in town every Tuesday, Friday and Sunday assisting Father Jensen with his ministries and pastoral duties. Fila felt more and more self-important with a renewed sense of the human spirit at its best in helping to care for the less fortunate. There was no violence here in Basalt– only an emotional satisfaction that there is a good side, a compassionate, rewarding side to human endeavors. The downside only came to light each evening before and during dinner when Zachary and George reported on all the bad news of the world as they listened to reports on their satellite phones. The world seemed forever in turmoil. And also, there was the daily issue of George's sly smiles and constant stares making Fila feel, feel what? She queried to herself -- *as a sex object?*

Eight

With more time on his hands now that his daytime life took on a series of routines that he became easily accustomed to, Zachary wanted for the first time to broach the subject of religion with Fila. He had never met anyone not a Christian or Jew. He had studied all the major religions in college and developed a keen interest in their comparisons and finding out where the real Truth lay. He understood that Christianity, Judaism, and Islam all seemed to believe in the same one God, yet a historical animosity existed, and apparent different interpretations of God's Word preyed on his mind. "On days you don't help Mom at St. Vincent's, Fila, can you go to our town library with me? Until everything settles back to normal, and until I can get a job or go to graduate school, I really want to study the world's religions more. I think you can help me with Islam, Fila."

"Sure, Zachary. I would enjoy doing that," Fila replied softly, a slight smile revealing her new warmth. This sincere young man had been so incredibly kind to her the last six months that she felt she would do anything in return. Well, almost anything. It wasn't difficult to sense -- Zachary was madly in love with Fila, but in controlling his emotions and knowing their ten-year age difference, he had to fight hard within himself every single day to hide his real feelings towards her.

"So you want to know more about the religion I grew up with Afghanistan, Islam, and I want to know more about your religion, Christianity. In fact, I want to learn more about all the major religions. I never could get over the fact that three religions all born in almost the same place in the world, Judaism, Christianity, and Islam all taught the belief in one almighty God, so it must be the same God, yet for so long there sometimes has been such animosity among them. Gosh, I …"

"I agree, animosity is the right word," chimed in Zachary, his face revealing widening enthusiasm. "So, let's start with you then me – Islam first."

During their twenty minute walk up Two Rivers Road from home to the Basalt library, Fila again turned towards that compelling sight as it suddenly came into view - that twin peaked, still snow capped mountain, Mt. Sopris, just as she had done with each walk to town center and St. Vincent's with Colleen and Grace.

"Look, Zachary. Isn't that beautiful? That mountain. Mt. Sopris."

"Yeah, incredible. We never get over it. A rare stand-alone mountain up here in the Rockies, and two peaks the same reach. Someday, I'll take you over there. You can climb to the top, no sweat, well except the final climb." Zachary took a fast peek and smiled. *She's great.* He could think it but just not ready to tell her.

The Basalt Regional Library is a modern structure with its expansive thirty- foot high, glass-windowed rear side facing Basalt Mountain. Certainly a unique and impressive view for a small town library building. It has multiple purposes from its book resources to young children's educational programs, language courses, to showing movies. A perfect spot for Fila and Zachary to pursue their quest for Truth.

"Okay, Zach, can I call you Zach? Fila smiled and sensed their ever-warming relationship as good friends. Zachary peered around the library to be sure no one was nearby listening.

"Sure, love it," he beamed.

"Well, I'll tell you what I was taught, and then we can explore more with what we can find in this library. So, some six hundred years after the time of Jesus, a man named Muhammad lived in a town, or small city, in the Arabian desert. He was born well off but orphaned early so then grew up of modest means, in a commercial center called Mecca. He observed that the better off there were often of treacherous, deceitful means, many tribal clans worshipping a number of pagan gods. Violence and corruption were rampant in and among the tribes and among the nomadic peoples living throughout the Arabian Peninsula. These were very conflicting times as Jews and Christians also lived there. Muhammad became a successful commercial trader but also was very intellectual and often visited a cave up in the mountains to reflect about things.

"Well, one day when he was about forty years old he went to the mountain area to think about life, and there an angel appeared to him, the angel Gabriel, who revealed to him the will and commands of the one God, Allah. He didn't write them down, but later scribes did from all his ongoing revelations and his teachings. This became the basis for the holy book of Islam, the Koran; Islam meaning total submission to Allah. The main point was that prophets before like Adam, Abraham, Moses, and Jesus all taught that there is but one God. Muhammad then became the last prophet sent by God to teach this concept."

Fila paused and took a deep breath interrupting her monologue on Muhammad. "Go on, go on," pleaded Zachary.

"Okay. So he had great difficulty and much conflict in convincing the pagan tribal leaders of his native Mecca this truth of one God already practiced by the Arabian Jews and Christians. Eventually, he and some of his followers, the Arabic name Muslims, moved some 300 miles away to an agricultural center called Medina where tribes of Jews and Christians lived among the pagans. He was able to unite the pagan tribal leaders, convert them to Islam, and develop a constitution that they could all live in peace together.

"Quite the statesman, huh?" Zachary smiled.

"Well, yes, but it gets complicated after that. There were lots and lots of skirmishes going on. Violent attacks were a norm out in the desert and among the settlements. It was almost ten years in Medina, I think around the year 630 that Muhammad was finally able to gather a strong force, some 10,000 men, and march upon antagonistic Mecca to finally quell the turmoil there. Surprisingly, the battle was relatively bloodless, and somehow he managed to convert all those pagans to the monotheistic new religion of Islam, the final word after Judaism and Christianity. He died just a couple of years later, but by that time his Islam had spread to all corners of the Arabian Peninsula."

"Wow!" What a guy!" Zachary's eyes filled with wonderment.

"That's just the beginning," as Fila edged forward in her chair by the light of the huge window. "The Word of God, the Koran, was about to explode East and West for the next five hundred years, partially because of widespread weaknesses in society elsewhere and also because of the fervor of the teachings of Islam were **total** – a complete way of life -- religious, political, society, economic. There was no separation. Religious law, Sharia law, everything about everything you do in your life all day long. How you act, how you behave and no separation between church and state. The main theme was noble --to be of good character, generous to the poor, to be righteous and go to Paradise in your afterlife, or to punishment in Hell if not. But the doctrine also included a concept you have heard of I'm sure, Zach, called Jihad, meaning to strive, to struggle, in the way of God."

Zachary frowned in silence, but leaned forward for more.

"So now the problems begin, haunting to this day, a thousand years plus later. Jihad has many interpretations. Without modifiers, it can mean to be warlike, meaning conversion to Islam by violent force if necessary. The Koran itself – many modern more liberal interpretations seeing some of the inherent contradictions in its expressions thereby allowing for compatibility with secular governments ... while others revert to a strict, fundamentalist interpretation thereby fostering the Muslim Brotherhood, the Wahhabis, and the violence of al Qaeda, the Taliban, ISIS. Today, some 1.6 billion followers, and still growing, from North Africa, the Middle East, Iran, India, Pakistan, China and the largest number, in Indonesia."

"Unbelievable," Zachary said calmly as Fila finally paused after such long but clear sentences. "You are better than my college professor in the lecture hall. We never learned that much background covering the Islam religion."

"So the big problem is still not yet reconciled -- it arose when Muhammad died naming no successor. Two different major sects arose almost immediately as a result of dissent between his closest descendants – the Sunnis, now more than eighty percent of the Muslim world and the Shias, less than twenty percent, but powerful. As I said, altogether over one and a half billion people today. The problem remains horrific, at times violent, between the two quarreling major sects and some of the minority sects in the Middle East. Iran and southern Iraq and parts of Syria being Shi'ite while northern Iraq, Egypt and Saudi Arabia being Sunni. And of course the harsh, radical, fundamentalist, often violent sects, the Wahhabi, the Taliban, and ISIS…. So this is what I grew up with and tried to escape to a new life.

"And always the disputes around Muhammad himself – sent by God as a prophet, a Holy Man, a moral man, a teacher of righteousness, yet he had a dozen wives, even married one when she was only six years old, had slaves, bought and sold them. You know Zach, slavery by far and away was not unique to the United States. A statesman he was, yes, but also a warrior. Maybe a truth is revealed to us Zach – I mean, 'it was the times.'

"Well, Zach, all this is why I am here today. We have a great religion in so many respects, most think obedience to God is really the ultimate message of peace, but Islam is also a troubled religion…. I learned that even you Christians had some violent times five hundred years ago sorting out the Protestant break from the Catholics, but I guess that was eventually resolved peacefully a long time ago. And of course there were the violent Crusades – Christians against Muslims over the so called 'Holy Land'."

"Right, true," Zachary interjected, " Christian violence is old history, except for the recent violence in Northern Ireland where the minority Irish Catholics sure didn't take to the dominance of the majority Protestants – those who are politically loyal to the rule of England, the United Kingdom," his voice dropping in an almost embarrassing tone. "But please, go on. What about you and Islam?"

"Well, in my native Afghanistan, a mostly tribal country torn apart since the time of that invading Greek three centuries before Christ, you know -- Alexander the Great -- we have been always divided. I was born in 1990 a year after the Russian army, who had been our occupiers since 1979, were pushed to withdraw by the fierce groups of guerilla fighters, the Mujahedeen. Can you believe, Zach, those insurgent groups were even supported by the United States, but the sad aftermath was that by 1994 the Islamist fundamentalist group called the Taliban became very strong politically and took over the country from the other Mujahedeen leaders. They moved our capital from Kabul to the southern city of Kandahar. I grew up in the middle. This was the dreaded Taliban, the violent men who kept women and dissidents down by force until the Americans came in after your 9/11/2001 attack and chased them east to Pakistan and south to their strongholds around Kandahar.

"This is what I witnessed as a young girl – the violence upon my economically poor and religiously moderate family.... I ... I was horrified, I grew up in fear ... but then with you Americans, yes you Americans, the very people I was taught to fear over this past year. When you Americans drove the Taliban out in 2003 while chasing those responsible for the 9/11 attack on America, Kabul was transformed. Kabul was renewed as our vibrant capital and suddenly young girls could enjoy relative peace, education, and work outside the home. As a young teenager, I felt blessed to have found both a job and a school to go to.

"But ten years later when the Americans left in 2014, the Taliban and their ruthlessness returned. So it all changed again when I was in my twenties and the Taliban returned to power. Same story I told Michael Reynolds. It was suppression, intimidation, violence, all over again. My friends and I lost everything. It was horrible. Two years later, I was ordered to marry an older Taliban fighter, but I think it would have been more as a sex slave, but just by pure luck, I ran into man conducting secret interviews to move to an island between the Arabian Sea and the Indian Ocean. He said he liked my looks, but whatever. The whole purpose was to escape the world of constant violence to an oasis of peace. It sounded too good to be true."

"But, I don't understand!" Zachary cried out. "You must have loved America when they removed the Taliban. When America later left, which is only natural that we could not stay forever, and the Taliban returned, you say you found peace on this island somewhere, then for God's sake Fila, how in the world could you come to attack us?" Clearly distraught, Zachary had raised his voice in the quiet library, incredulous to what he just heard.

Fila looked him right in the eye trying to calm him, replying in a soft reassuring voice. "I will tell you, Zach, I will tell you another time. It's a whole 'nother story.... I am so sorry. Please believe me, I have no quarrel with your country or you Americans now. I can't thank you enough for your kindness."

"I can sense you are confused, Fila. I think every normal person in the world desires love and peace – maybe that's 99.9% of all of us. It's that .1% that you are talking about causing all the trouble – the Taliban, ISIS, certain corrupt world leaders, the mentally imbalanced in this country that suddenly go berserk and commit murder, the...."

His voice trailed off. Fila stared at him in awe, and in sorrow. Nothing made sense.

In the warmer springtime weather of 2022, everyone became busier than ever. Electricity and water from the public utilities were still not flowing, so food production was still issue number one. There was now the tending to existing gardens in early bloom, clearing and tilling vacant land for new areas to plant seeds of all kinds, the greater availability of game in the mountains to be hunted, while fishing for trout in the nearby streams and rivers became more accessible as the winter snow was melting.

Spring fever also stirred the spirit of another person twenty miles down valley from Basalt. Like Michael Reynolds, Zachary and George Gelayes, the young man named John Striver in Glenwood Springs could not get the image of that alluring women out of his mind -- the enchanting eyes and soft voice of that stranger who passed through many months ago. *Could she really have gone to Independence and survived the winter? No way – that would be a miracle,* he thought to himself.

On a beautiful Sunday morning in June, John was attending the family gas station until such time his Dad could take over in the late morning upon his return from church services. There had been very little activity at the station over the winter, but now business was picking up. Additional supplies of propane gas had arrived to run the electric generator which provided power for electric vehicles and also to power the pumps to pull gasoline from the new supplies provided to their tanks. Glenwood Springs was an important stopping point for essential traffic along Interstate 70, so the federal government had designated it as a critical location for ample rationing of fuel supplies.

"John, take the rest of the day off, son," his father beckoned. "I'm good now. Go enjoy yourself. You worked hard this week, and I need you here first thing tomorrow."

"Okay, yeah Dad, I can do that." John was in his mid twenties, medium height, about 5'10", a little stocky, light skin, long, straight blond hair often falling over half his somewhat chubby baby face. He had gained great accolades as an outstanding linebacker on his high school football team but never felt the ambition to go to college. He had several girlfriends over the last ten years but never cemented a lasting relationship. The girls all had thought him quite cute but never very sincere or dedicated to anything special.

Today was different – his masculine instinct arising. He still had an old Buick given to him by his father when he was just sixteen. It had a full tank of gas. He made a quick decision. He figured now is the time. *I can drive up 82 and be in Independence in an hour. I'll look for her til I find her.*

Route 82 had few cars or trucks on the highway as he proceeded up the gradual incline at 65 mph. His could feel his chest beating heavy now as his excitement grew. He was on a mission. It felt good. After twenty miles, he could see the cut off for Carbondale on the right, a view of Mt. Sopris, now green half way up and appearing grayish towards the rocky top with still some snow on its very peaks. Then little Jebel on the left followed by a traffic light stop at the Two Rivers Road intersection on the left, never noticing the houses wedged in between the start of that road and the base of Basalt Mountain. It was another mile to the main entrance road into Basalt, and then another twenty miles right into the heart of the main street through Aspen. *If she was smart she woulda' stayed right here for the winter. No skiing but what a great town.*

After leaving Aspen and during the next ten miles up to the 13,000 ft. summit at the Continental Divide, Independence Pass, the road narrowed and wandered through thick groves of beautiful forest. John stopped just before the summit at a large clearing off the road where several cars were parked. *This must be the old miners' settlement.* He soon found out the car owners were all there to fish for trout, that there were no old signs about, and that no one knew of just where that 150 year old tent city might have been, even though this spot seemed to be the logical location. *She never would have survived here anyway over the winter,* he thought to himself over and over again as he explored around. Back in his car he drove hurriedly back down to Aspen and then spent the next hour just wandering slowly up and down every street just staring at every person he could see. No girl or woman came close to what he envisioned in his mind – his clear image of that totally unique beauty. Slowly back down 82, looking, looking but hardly anyone on the roadside.

Then why not? *I have the time.* It seemed he was under a spell. He made the right hand turn into the next town -- Basalt. Crawling up and down the two short streets, he could see only a handful of inhabitants were out walking. Nothing. But then the route became peculiar -- coming back down the main street to get back to Route 82, one has to bear slightly left and go past the library towards the highway. Not paying full attention in his growing frustration, John kept driving his Buick straight ahead. Now he was on Two Rivers Road but still headed down the slope towards Glenwood Springs. About almost a mile down the narrow passage he could see in the distance that the road ran into Route 82 at a traffic light.

"Wait," he said out loud to himself. All of a sudden there were three females walking together towards that intersection. They were all wearing jeans, blouses and loose sweaters. They all looked good to him. Actually, they were just walking home from Sunday Mass and from helping out at their church. When he slowed the car to a crawl, they sensed the vehicle behind them and quickly moved to a single file to let him pass. As he unhurriedly passed each one, he could see they were of different ages – the first a middle aged woman, maybe 50, then a girl, maybe a young teenager, and then, and then! It was her. *It's her! Jesus!*

His mind raced. He felt joy. He felt excitement. He could not think straight and suddenly became so nervous, he momentarily hesitated on the gas pedal, almost bringing his vehicle to a complete stop, stared fleetingly at Fila who returned the glance directly into his eyes, and then he nervously stepped on the gas pedal and roared ahead towards the nearby traffic light that was now green. He didn't know what to do next, so he just sat at the green light and waited for it to turn red, all the time turning his head and eyes back towards the three females.

"That guy just didn't seem right. Wait right here, girls, and let him go," Colleen pleaded.

"Yeah, he looked strange didn't he, staring at us, but I have never seen him before, Mom," replied Grace. "Did you recognize him?"

"No dear, and I don't like strangers staring at us like that."

As the old Buick finally pulled ahead and made the right hand turn at the light, Grace made an attempt to lighten the situation. "Okay, let's make it home but maybe that guy just happened to think we were a good looking trio of broads and wanted a close look. Well at least at beautiful Fila here."

"That's not funny Grace," Colleen replied. "He's out of sight now. Let's get home…. And I'm telling you in no mixed words, my young teenager – never get lured or pulled into a car by a strange man. The world's not all pure out there." After hearing Colleen's strong words of caution to her daughter, Fila looked down, her face sullen, puzzled. She had recognized that face and didn't like his stares, but couldn't quite place him. The three continued their walk home but now at an accelerated pace.

John was not sure what to do next. If he went back to them, he knew that he wouldn't know what to say to her. *Hello, remember me? Where did you spend the winter? Do you know there is a guy from Denver looking for you?* He had not thought all that out in advance in case he did find her on his mission. And she was not alone. Who are the others? *Geez, I was so lucky to find her the first time up here, but...* He realized now that maybe he just had an urge to see her. So he simply drove at half speed all the way home, going over and over in his mind that maybe he will find her again now that he knows about where she is, and next time maybe she will be alone, and he will have the right words to say.

———————•——————

The summer days flowed by. Everyone was busy. The inhabitants of the Roaring Fork Valley found little time for recreation. Providing sufficient food for all was still the priority, and that task was handled quite well. Only the town of Aspen felt helpless. The beautifully situated resort had experienced a tremendous resurgence the last fifty years due to its four terrific ski mountains and its summer music festivals. All that was missing in the year 2022. Aspen became a virtual ghost town. It was down valley towards Basalt, Carbondale, and Glenwood Springs where the locals learned to survive and almost thrive. Farms and ranches were the play now, not recreation.

In Denver, Michael found himself fully occupied helping to find solutions to the national crisis, but of course still thinking of Fila every night. In Glenwood Springs, John Striver found time on his days off to drive his old Buick up to Two Rivers Road searching unrewardingly for a glimpse of Fila again, of course thinking about meeting her in his daydreams every day. In Basalt, George was continually fighting his urge to simply give Fila a hug, although his imagination rose to much lustier intentions. Zachary kept himself busy with a variety of tasks aimed at preparing for the next winter's stresses of his family and town folks especially in the event electric power was not yet restored. Even so, his mind searched for more time to spend with his alluring housemate, the beautiful Fila, to explore more religions with her. Young developing Grace, getting more and more second looks from the Basalt boys, increasingly sensed these male-female attractions. And she could not fail to miss the looks that even our own brother and father as well as town boys and men gazed at every opportunity towards this mysterious foreign visitor. She continuously thought to herself: *What is it about Fila that is so attractive to these men? As my roommate, I see her naked, and yes she truly is a beautiful looking woman in all ways, but I think there must be even more, some mystique in those eyes.*

Nine

A s summer turned to autumn and then early winter 2023, Fila found more and more time to return to the library and read as much as she could find on all the world's major religions. She discovered some were part philosophy as well, beyond just the mysteries of the super naturals. She also began the endeavor to learn who the most significant philosophers were over the course of recorded history and learn of their take on life as well. But first, the religions.

Not long after the start of the new year, Zachary was able to find some time between hunting expeditions with his father to join Fila and make it a joint venture to the library. At their next enlightenment session together, Zachary could not wait to get started. "Now it is my turn to tell you about Christianity, now over two billion followers even larger than the worldwide Muslim population. But first, we should cover Judaism, since as you know Jesus was a Jew, and that religion came first, maybe starting some two thousand years before Christ."

"Wait. First Zach, tell me why you said 'Christ'. I know his name was Jesus but why is he also 'Jesus Christ'? I never understood that."

Helping the two of them get comfortable sitting on two chairs by the huge window facing the base of Basalt mountain,

Zachary seemed delighted at Fila's first question. There were only two other visitors strolling the library and only one employee behind the large counter located midway in the structure. Smiling, Zachary answered her question with authority. Yes 'Jesus' is his name and 'Christ' is his title to his disciples and to us Christians. In Hebrew it means 'messiah' but of course the Jews do not believe that he was the true messiah, the true deliverer of the Jewish people. 'Christ' to us means 'The Chosen One' or 'The Anointed One', so to us he is the son of God chosen or anointed to teach us of everlasting life by believing in him."

"Okay, got it," said Fila. "Go on."

"Right. So Judaism goes way back and what we were taught in college is that the historical record is quite incomplete and can be confusing. After the big agricultural revolution some ten thousand years ago, which allowed man to really advance with language and thinking by allowing some to stay put and communicate, one of the main areas benefiting was the temperate climate areas of the eastern side of the Mediterranean, like Persia and to what is now Iraq, Syria, and certainly Egypt. The Egyptians and Babylonians were progressing quite well a few thousand years before Jesus.

"It is believed an Arab in the desert named Abraham was approached by God and directed to find a promised land a little to his west called Canaan or Judah. He went there, and that is the beginning of the story of the Jewish Old Testament. Abraham believed he had a Covenant, a requirement, to teach obedience to his fellow man to experience God's presence in human events. His sons and many ancestors were the key to the whole story, at least shortly after Adam and Eve and the creation of the our world was briefly explained."

"Was Abraham the beginning of belief in one God, the

opposite of paganism? Wasn't he the first Prophet?" Fila said, edging forward in her chair.

"Yes and yes," Zachary replied, "and to teach that the one God's purpose was the establishment of peace and well-being in the universe and within mankind, but you know, the start up of that religion had a tough time ... yeah funny, right through to today. It's thought maybe that beginning was some two thousand years before Christ. Abraham's people were soon exiled to Babylon and then later sent to Egypt, while maybe some thirteen hundred years before Christ, the second Jewish Prophet, Moses, delivered them out of exile and back to Israel. He is the one who went to the top of Mt. Sinai and received the Ten Commandments from God, the basis of instructing the Jews of proper behavior. You want me to name them, Fila?"

"No, no, I have heard them many times. Remember, in Islam, Abraham, Moses, and Jesus are the religion's great Prophets before the last one, Muhammad."

"Okay, now to differentiate Judaism from Christianity, the Old Testament paints a picture of many lesser prophets who were divinely inspired to warn the Israelites that when a person or community failed in their religious responsibilities found in their holy book, the Torah, and in God's Ten Commandments, then those persons and communities could face punishment from God. It could happen on earth and also in a final judgment, whenever that is to be, I think when the true prophet comes, the choice between eternal heaven and eternal hell."

Fila spoke up, fully alert. "I'm getting the feeling ... like Islam, God is recognizing and allowing man to have enough free will to be disorderly, disobedient, but then atonement is being offered through a solid belief and a turn to follow the holy rules...."

"Exactly!" Zachary interjected. "That's it. A moral God is

calling for order and obedience but man doesn't always follow the righteous path and can be punished, but he does have a path offered for redemption. And while the religion accepts an immortal soul, a spirit, within everyone, there seems to be a split among different Jewish sects as to what eventually happens to all those souls. I'm a little puzzled by that."

"Well, at least," responded Fila. "It seems the Jews of Israel, although very much at odds with Islamic Iran, have something in common with that Persian theology – both cultures view their religions as the supreme ethnical way of living – their set of basic beliefs and values."

"Yeah, I guess you're right Fila, maybe that's true about all religions, and yet the Jews think they are the one Chosen people. They are a very strong ethnic and religious community. They want their state of Israel to be both. They believe they are the one's chosen to deliver God's message – obedience to the path of righteousness, rebellion an option but punishment and possible atonement can follow."

Fila smiled, "Well, amazing that with all those hardships of contesting for their promised land, their exiles to Babylon and Egypt, and then I know their spread to all of Europe and Russia and America, and their mass extinctions by the Nazis … it's amazing that they stick together so well to this day."

"Yeah, you're right, again" Zachary concurred with a shrug. "I give them a lot of credit for their fortitude. As the land of Judah was always in the crossing path of warring factions, the Jews always seemed to be in a state of dispersion – like you said, throughout the Middle East, Eastern and Western Europe, Russia, the U.S. It's thought their book, the Torah, kept them bound together. Amazing history -- great courage. After two World Wars and after the defeat of the thousand year Muslim Ottoman Empire, and after the area's subsequent control by

Britain, and after the Jewish population loss of millions by the Nazis ... finally, the United Nations in 1948 gave the Jews their independent nation of Israel.

"But! They were almost immediately decimated by the many millions of Muslims surrounding their new borders -- a very small area, but they survived, and then when later attacked in 1967, the new Israelites had the strength to actually win more land, and gain greater security with support from the United States. Darn, the situation was not and is still not settled. The Muslim Palestinians surrounding them and within still make claim to the same land. No settlement, no lasting peace."

"Tragic for the world," Fila's eyes expressing empathy. "There are not that many Palestinians, and they don't get much support from the Muslim nations around them, and I read there are only some six million Jews in Israel. What's the solution? Is it the land, the religions, the cultures?"

"I don't know," Zachary replied looking down. "The Jews lost six million in the Nazi extermination, and maybe there are another six million here in the United States. Probably only another million spread around the world. I don't know the answer."

Again her face lighting up, Fila replied with a slight smile, "Look, at least we know that those guys Abraham and Moses must have done amazingly great jobs. Through all that hardship, the Jews have stuck together and their faith survives. So maybe America survives too from the likes of my terrible people, my so-called friends who attacked you ... and from a very lost Fila." On those words surprisingly uttered from her own mouth, she suddenly looked down. The smile evaporated, with a tear coming to her eye.

Zachary quickly reached out, grabbed her hand firmly with

his, and with his other hand gave her forearm a strong squeeze. The end of the lessons for today. They walked home in silence.

———————•●———————

A week later, while Fila was clearing breakfast dishes from the table, Zachary whispered out to her. "Hey, I have some time this afternoon. How bout to the library and Christianity?" Fila looked briefly at him and gave a quick nod approvingly.

Still seated finishing his coffee, George seemed engrossed in something on a large piece of paper, but caught the offer and acceptance. "Son, I have noticed these walks with Fila to the library you two take. Not often, but you up to something?"

Taken by surprise, Zachary now standing, simply looked blank back at his father. George continued, "Zach, I know we all have taken this girl in and she has been very helpful here, but we still don't know much 'bout her and her background. We have to be careful. Remember she came here to destroy us. And I know she is quite attractive too. I see you stare. Now don't get any ideas. She is almost ten years older than you and …"

"Dad, Dad, listen," Zachary countered softly so no one else could hear. "I know all that. She is just confused, tormented about her mission here, and she wants to learn all the good things different religions teach us. We're exploring library books and talking. She wants to be helped. You know I studied religion in school. I …"

"Hogwash. You and your mom believe all that crazy stuff. Why is the world so much of a mess even after all these horrible wars, and now look what's happened to us. Where is that loving god of yours, huh? It's a fiction, son. Those religious leaders like the big politicians and dictators around the world just want power. They just want the goodies that come with being in charge, until they lose in the next fight. Just follow the one good thing your religion taught: 'do unto others as you would have them do unto you'. If we all did just that, things would be fine."

"Dad, it's simply faith. There's no obvious proof except to some, but I am not going to argue with you. Let us have our personal faith in a higher calling."

"I don't begrudge that, son. You know I love and respect you and your mom, and you should believe as you wish. Just be careful with that girl, that's all I'm saying."

"Got it, Dad, got it." Zachary hustled away, quickly forgetting his father's warning.

———— •———

At the library that afternoon, Zachary again found two chairs by the big window and made sure Fila was seated close and directly across from him so he could clearly look right at her. He subconsciously always felt exhilarated when he could look closely into her large green eyes. At the dining table and here at the library were the best opportunities.

"So now Fila, my religion – Christianity. You know we are bigger than yours. Over two billion followers -- all over the world, but especially Europe and the Americas. When Jesus was born two thousand years ago, six hundred years before Muhammad, Israel was ruled by the Romans, part of The Roman Empire. Most inhabitants were poor. So the first message to you is that Jesus had two audiences. The first was the Jewish religious leaders whom Jesus thought were giving a weak message. The second was to the many plain folks who suffered and needed that key ingredient, that great stimulus – hope! …. So when my college prof had us reading *The Greatest Story Ever Told* and asked us what was Jesus' greatest message, I was so happy that I was the first to shout out 'ever lasting life', and the prof looked at me and smiled and said 'right!'." Zachary looked at Fila seeking just a little approbation.

"Ha," she chimed in. "So the hope was the promise of everlasting life if you believed in Jesus."

"Right on, Fila, and what Jesus strongly implied but never clearly stated was that he was actually the Son of God sent to deliver that message to quote 'whomever believes in me'. So today, we Christians look at all three as part of one – first, the spirit of God and that which is within us, second, God, and third, his Son, Jesus. But as much as Jesus performed miracles and helped the disadvantaged, he had a hard time convincing the elite high priests, many appointed by the Roman governors, of his message to get back to God's teachings. In effect, he only attracted a dozen loyal ongoing followers, his apostles, the disciples, the ones who tell his story in our New Testament, a book added to the Old Jewish Testament as our complete Bible but without all the old warnings to behave. The new one is more about love, hope, and forgiveness. So then in fact, when the tide of the priests turned against Jesus and the claims about him as the Son of God, they got the approval of the Romans, and he was sentenced to death. The Jews never believed Jesus was their true Messiah, the one who would be the savior of the Jewish people and who would rule in the world in days to come. Carrying his cross through the streets, up a hill, to be crucified until death next to some common criminals, we Christians say God allowed this so that Jesus could rise again three days later, our Easter. We believe that his death and resurrection was his way of expressing his love for us, our salvation to everlasting life if we believe in him as the way to the Lord."

"Fascinating," said Fila. "But then without support from the Romans or the Jewish elite, only from that first dozen, how did the religion survive and grow?"

"Quite a fascinating story, Fila, a remarkable tale. Three of Jesus' disciples later put his story to writing – Matthew, Mark and Luke -- the beginning part of our New Testament. The mother of Jesus, Mary, was a virgin, although married. Jesus was conceived by God's doing, and Mary is still adorned to this day; statues and paintings of her holding her child are in our churches and homes everywhere. But for many years this story appealed only to the impoverished masses, not their well-to-do leaders, because its message of love, forgiving, and salvation gave the common people the gift of hope.

"One of Jesus' disciples, Peter, went to Rome and established the first Christian church, and later became referred to as our first Pope, 'father' in Latin, and renamed Saint Peter. Some thirty years after the crucifixion of Jesus he too was crucified -- by the Roman emperor, Nero. You know, the early Christians had a tough time until three hundred years later when the pagan emperor, Constantine, converted and sanctioned the religion. He also moved the head of the Roman Empire to a city renamed Constantinople, now Istanbul, and after all that, today you see two Christian Catholic sects -- the main Roman to the west and the Orthodox to the east. And a third branch formed some fifteen hundred years after Jesus. Some northern Europeans objected to the supreme authority of the Roman Pope, and after bitter disputes and even wars, the Protestant branch evolved, and later with its multiple denominations, like Episcopalian, Presbyterian, Lutheran and so on. In any Christian church, you will always see a crucifixion cross with the body of Jesus nailed to it. He is our savior. Our belief in Him is our path to everlasting life."

"That's nice, Zach. That's nice. I can admire you for your faith. To me, for a long time now, I just haven't known what to believe. We were taught Jesus was simply another prophet among many. Christianity sounds like a more peaceful religion than Islam without your Jihad, but all these centuries of violence. World War II with seventy million dying – weren't the Nazis' Christians? And the rise of atheistic Communism – where do all the Communists go when they die? Do they have a chance for salvation like the Jews, Christians, and Muslim? And what do your priests teach you why God allows all this violence? Free will? "

"Fila, Fila, stop," Zachary interjected softly. "We don't know where non Christians go at death. You don't know where non-Muslims go at death. Where is Heaven for them? And our priests don't know why our God allows all this violence, but they teach us He has a long-term plan that is good. Can you believe that Christians, Muslims and Jews all believe in the same one God, so maybe there is one heaven, but who knows about the other three billion people on earth. For centuries Muslims expanded their religion east and west with Jihad, sometimes violently. Christians also expanded with traveling evangelical priests, especially to the Americas, some to China, thankfully often peaceful. The point is to accept the civil order of a religious society, whereas societies like the Communists of China or now secular Russia have their own versions of a rule of law so as to preserve order. Atheistic Communist governments in Russia and China allowed religion to exist, but not flourish, just not to upset the traditions of those masses of people the communist leaders consider to be disillusioned. Belief in an afterlife is a matter of faith for each of us Christians. We believe in what we choose; we are not forced into anything. Freedom of choice; freedom of religion."

"And America has what? A secular government with voluntary religions among the governed? Where is your guidance?" Fila responded rather forcefully, demanding answers.

"Yes, that's right. Our government follows the U.S. Constitution, written by our Founding Fathers after breaking from the King of England in 1776. It credits God for the equality of men and falls back on Judeo-Christian rules of behavior in writing law, but keeps government out of declaring a state religion and guarantees religious freedom. We have civilian laws to keep our order. You as a Muslim are free to live in this country and follow your faith, but the only caveat is our separation of state and religion, so you have to accept our Constitution as supreme and not proclaim Sharia Law here."

"So you have churches, synagogues, mosques, Buddhist temples?"

"All of that…. From the first Christian churches of different sects, different denominations, which still prevail, but the others followed. And we have no violent Sunni/Shite problem like you told me about."

"Like the mentally ill and the places of worship here – they are both 99.9% peaceful?"

"You could say that, Fila." Zachary sat back in his chair looking quite satisfied where this discussion was going.

Fila continued. "And the natives here before the white man – you call them Indians because I read Columbus thought he had discovered India. What do they believe?"

"Zachary sat back up. "Native Americans, although they originally migrated from Asia…. Another time, Fila, another time."

"Yes, that's what your mother told me too," her eyes pleading at Zachary's.

With the cold winter days limiting outside tasks, Zachary and Fila found more time to walk to the library and continue their discussions. The building was able to obtain some heat in the afternoons through its emergency generator system, and the huge window provided sufficient light. On days Fila was not busy with Colleen at the Catholic Church, she searched through library books which would give some insight into the thinking of philosophers considered the world's greatest over recorded history. She craved answers as to why people act as they do.

"I'm so glad you are talking to her about our religion," Colleen said to her son after dinner one evening out of everyone else's listening. "She is doing us a great service at the church and in the community. She's dedicated. I pray she is now seeing Americans, and Christians, as gracious and peaceful."

"Right, Mom, she is a very smart person. We wish 'peace to the world' every Christmas and like to believe our Christianity is a religion of peace. That's certainly the message of Jesus, but you know, most Muslims are also taught Islam is a religion of 'peace', that the violent sects among the religion are simply out of the mainstream, and wrong. The universal call for peace, yet the all too many conflicts leading to violence, continuing from the time of all these religions getting their start so long ago … well, that's where she is confused. Remember the story of Cassius Clay, a young black boxer raised in a city where blacks were treated second class, refusing to go to Vietnam and be asked to kill yellow-skinned Asians. So he was legally punished for awhile, but he converted to Islam as the religion of 'peace', changed his name to Muhammad Ali, became a great champion, and then upon retirement became a tremendous advocate for the disadvantaged."

"I do remember. Well, we just have to keep our hopes alive for justice eventually everywhere and that in God's mysterious way, a way that we don't really understand, the true path to heaven is through peace within each of us and through our belief in Jesus. Yes, things are often bad on earth given our free will and the forces of nature, but we pray for peace on earth and are given a path to reach the Lord in Heaven. Despite your father's influence, Zachary, I am so happy you have that faith," Colleen responded as she reached out and gave her grown son a warm embrace.

Ten

"This is really hard to understand, Zach, not being familiar enough with the very long period of Asian history." Fila appear to look bewildered, three open books in front of her on a library desk by the big window. Spring was in the air, but the two could not stay away from the peace and quiet of the Basalt library.

"I know," Zach replied with a sigh. All the different interpretations over the years, all the emperors and Chinese dynasties with different emphasis. Taoism is tough for Westerners to fully grasp. It looks like we have to grasp all three to understand better – Buddhism, Hinduism, and Taoism. And the there is Confucianism too. They all seem to come together, to blend, somehow."

"Well, I think part of it is that India and China today have some three billion people," Fila replied. "With the rest of southeast Asia and Japan, half the world's population. I guess so populous, there must be many, many different local sects and practices."

"Okay, right. So let's just start with the Chinese, not all of Asia, knowing that India was mainly Hinduism and Islam, even though the Buddha started there, with Islam primarily moving to Pakistan in recent history, and a little Buddhism slipping into China."

Looking somewhat exasperated, Fila exclaimed, "Wait! I'm confused. Asia – China and also Vietnam, Korea, and Japan too? How about Islamic Indonesia? And aren't all these religions also philosophies too? Start over Zach."

"Okay, yes and yes," Zachary leaned forward acting like the current professor of world's religions. Let's just start with early China, a few hundred years before Jesus Christ. We'll come back to India and the rest later. The Chinese ways eventually spread to the rest of Asia. Two primary religions developed before Christ – Taoism and Confucianism. Some Buddhism later crept in as a third tradition some 100 years after Christ when missionaries from India introduced Buddhism into China.

"So, this guy Confucius was a real man, some 500 years before Christ. The Chinese had mythical leaders some couple hundred years before Christ that they thought to be wise and just, but now order in their society was breaking down. Sound like a familiar theme? Confucius thought that to regain order out of the chaos that each man, not just the rulers, should be encouraged to quote 'learn' -- that a new code of conduct should be the norm for everyone. You could say it was mostly a new philosophy, but somewhat a religion in its reverence towards an undefined 'heaven'. The thousands of temples built throughout all of China were not really religious but were built to teach Confucius' theme of 'love of men', to be 'virtuous'. His writings about this became known as the Classics, and Chinese rulers adopted the urgings as official state code. Of course, over the next two thousand years different schools of thought and different rulers all placed different emphasis on the codes of conduct, with Taoism also coming into play."

"Confusing, Zach," Fila sat back with an unusual frown on that pretty face.

"A little," countered Zachary, "but not so much. You'll see. Taoism was more on the informal, accepting, joyful side while Confucianism more on the stern, formal side. Somewhat complementary when practiced together actually."

"Okay, go on. We'll compare what you were taught in school with what I'm learning here from these books," Fila said, lighting up now.

"Right, okay. So here's a good thing. You must know, or maybe you don't – you see Chinese people acting so polite to each other and to strangers. That comes from generations of practicing that the Confucian interplay between and among people should be courteous. Again the principles of love as a life pattern. The idealism of humanism put into play. To Confucianism, the family is all-important. The family is the rock between the individual and the state. It proceeds in steps. It starts with the learning of the individual, to seek knowledge then become wise, to construct the superior man, then he creates the strong family, then he can wisely govern the state, and finally he can bring peace to the world.... Neat, huh, Fila?"

"Got it. What I read too. But I missed their understanding of evil. I don't understand this *chi* stuff."

Zachary continued. "Well, you've heard of the practice of *Tai Chi*? There is the inner nature of man, an inner force called *chi*. It can be inherently good or it can be bad. If your *chi* is not cultivated through learning, through enlightenment, it can create evil in man. That's it -- that's why there are bad things on earth." Zachary looked satisfied with his expertise.

"Too simple, but too common. Back to your story of Adam and Eve, right? Or Islam, if we are not totally obedient to Allah's rules of behavior, we can act in evil ways…. I think I need more," Fila responded with a renewed frown.

"Fila, we can live with this," Zachary reacted sharply. "Jews and Christians are taught the Golden Rule: 'Do unto others as you would have them do unto you.' It was actually Confucius who was quoted by his many disciples as saying 'Do not do to others what you would not want others to do to you'. Why can't we all live with that?"

A long silence pursued as Fila bowed her head. She spoke so softly Zachary had to strain to hear her. "But we don't. Look at me. Why did I come here with hate in my heart? To kill, to be evil. Where is this God? I thought I was to do good, not bad. I was taught America is evil even though they had helped my Afghanistan for a while. Where is this universal moral code? Where is this love of men? This golden rule? Why don't I have it? My *chi* is bad? My free will is evil? I'm not obedient to Allah's rules? I'm not learned and wise? What's wrong with me, and so many others? Are we all born evil, and then have to be taught to be good?"

Zachary responded speaking as softly, rising and putting his arms and hands out to her shoulders. "That's the point, Fila, that's the point of all of this. We don't really know the answer to that, but we have to try to understand the inner nature of man, and then to correct our shortcomings. We simply don't have all the answers yet. Let's just go home now."

———— • ————

As early Spring 2023 had approached, winter supplies of meat, fish, and firewood were still copious, but the family supplies of potatoes and vegetables had run out. It was time for planting in Coleen's very efficient garden. Success -- the winter wheat she had planted the previous autumn was beginning to sprout. Time now to get the potato and vegetable planting on the move. The three ladies took to those tasks while George and Zachary continued to hunt and fish. The days were tiring; the evenings a little talk before turning in about the condition of Basalt, the Roaring Fork Valley, and whatever they could learn from their cell phones about the nation's progress, especially in restoring the electrical grid. The local distribution of electrical current was improving – a few hours a day spread to more homes and businesses. No television or radio yet. Supplies by boat to seaports on the coasts continued to pour in, and the vibrant trucking industry continued its herculean task of distributing essentials throughout the nation. Michael Reynolds remained one busy guy.

Nonetheless, Zachary and Fila found Sunday afternoons after church services the best time that they could escape to the library, again and again. They found somewhat limited volumes on Taoism, Buddhism, and Hinduism, but fortunately the library had a full set of the old Encyclopedia Britannica, a 1976 printing, which had been donated to it by an elderly gentleman the very day the library had opened. "Okay, let's finish up with China before we move to India and their three religions. We discussed one of the Chinese primary religions, Confucianism, but not the other, Taoism. And also we learned some Buddhism imported from India later became an important influence upon the Chinese culture," Zachary said as they sat by the big library windows and mutually set down their books.

"Yes," Fila replied. "I even just learned some regions of very western China had a very substantial number of Muslims settle there while in the east a good number of Chinese became Christians, converted by Western missionaries. But of course the atheistic Communist Party has minimized all that, not sure by what means though. But as we said before, the Communists can't fool too much with the philosophical side of Chinese customs developed over many centuries from the three religions you mentioned."

"Yeah, we're not gonna know it all, but at least we'll know the basics so we can make some judgments here."

"That's what I'm looking for, Zach. I want to understand what we're all doing here on earth … and what I've done." Fila dropped her head, looking solemn.

"Hey, cheer up, Miss, me too. We're going to learn why we're the same and why we're different, and why we all just can't get our act together.… There was a not so smart guy a few years ago here who said a pretty smart thing after a little rough encounter, like 'why can't we all just get along?'"

Fila looked up, and returned Zachary's warm smile.

"Okay, Taosism. Here's my take from what I read," Zachary's bright enthusiasm taking hold. "As we learned before, Taoism is the more accepting, carefree side of life complementing the more austere, purposeful side of Confucianism. It's the positive attitude. It's personal. Looks like I understand it as a combination of historical customs and culture, religion, and philosophy. All three. Seems to have spread through all of east Asia sometime around 400 years before Christ, and unlike being complementary to Confucianism, it seems somewhat contradictory to the introduction of Buddhism into China, which downplays the individual ego and makes the physical world seem illusory."

"Zach, I don't see anywhere that Tao was a person."

"No, Tao means 'way'. I see here it says a code of behavior and a doctrine. But it seems uplifting. It brings everything into balance – heaven and earth, man and nature united. It's like magic – a universal force, returning all to its purest form, pushing us humans to find wisdom to be in harmony with the universe. It sounds exciting, Fila, teaching this yin/yang stuff with everything pulsating, complementary energies, nothing static."

"Hey, I like it, but where is good and evil in all this?" Fila queried.

"You know, I'm not exactly sure. I think human behavior is supposed to be exemplary. The religious part teaches a vital force in us that can be immortal and go to heaven. There seem to be many gods, none ruling over the earth, and many sects, and many significant interpretations over the centuries, including as a form of mysticism that would make it more of a philosophy. There were various books, not one like we have.... Looked at as a philosophy then your question of good and peace must come from their approach of using solitary meditation to gain knowledge and become perfect, in a complete rhythm with nature and eventually become what they call 'a pure spirit'."

Exasperated, Fila chimed in, "Okay, that's great for the dedicated individual. That person will do no harm to others, but for the masses who take it less seriously and as you said less demanding then Confucianism and Buddhism, where is the common moral code not to commit violence upon another?"

"Wait," Zachary exclaimed. "We said the east Asians - China, Vietnam, Korea, Japan - have a blend of all these religions and philosophies. So yes, the dedicated wise individual devoted himself to wisdom and perfection while the common man has the blend of all these religions and philosophies instructing him to at least be orderly in his daily life."

A moment of reflection, a period of silence, and then Fila countered. "So it's just a few that are disorderly? Setting their own rules of behavior, capable of violence upon one another or upon the orderly? Why is that?"

"We need a break, Fila. Let's take a walk."

It was another three Sundays before the two could break away and resume their learning at the library. On the walk up Two Rivers Road, as usual Fila stopped and stared as Mt. Sopris came into view.

"Still fascinated by that sight, huh Fila?"

The twin peaks, Zach. I would just like to park myself in between someday," Fila replied.

"Yeah, you know, the peaks are exactly the same height. Amazing. Now look, the snow on top is almost fully melted. The tree line near the rocky summits is in full view. Beautiful. So sure, we can go there. My friend Ed Wise has a jeep and he has been able to find some gas lately, so we can drive to the base of the trail and hike up as soon as full summer is here."

"Would love that, Zach. Thanks." Fila took one long last look before the two continued their walk to the library.

———— • ————

"Okay, enough of East Asia, let's go to India. Just about the same population as China, so the two together must be somewhere around forty percent of the world's total population. So this guy Buddha is a big influence," Zachary began.

"Yes, true, but I read here India's primary religion is Hinduism, and there was such a big mixture of conflicting Muslims of the Islamic faith that after independence was won from England in 1947, the nation of Pakistan was created directly north of India for the Muslims. And all these movements …"

"Well, right," Zachary interrupted. "I see the many differences in politics and all the civil disobedience movements characterizing the region, but I think, Fila, we'll stick to the religions."

"Mister Buddha, go!" Fila said smiling as she sat back comfortably in her chair. "I'm all ears."

Zachary retuned the grin. "Ya know, I learned some of this stuff in college ... but it was good to have this encyclopedia here too, so just listen up, girl. Your real Mister Buddha lived some 2500 years ago. That's 500 years before my Jesus Christ and over 1000 years before your Muhammad. He was actually a wealthy prince who was transformed into a wandering holy man after wondering why those outside his palace were so suffering. He spent time praying and meditating until finally he came to understand what he believed to be the three basic truths about life. Not on top of a mountain like Moses and Muhammad, but under a poplar-fig tree. He became enlightened, and then he was actually given the title Buddha, the Enlightened One. Want to hear these Universal Truths, Miss Fila?"

Fila's smile grew larger as she nodded her head approvingly.

"And over the next many years teaching, he expanded the Three Universal Truths into the Four Noble Truths and then added Eight Guides. Neat, huh?"

"What a guy!"

"Okay, Universal," said Zachary. "First, everything in life is ever changing and nothing is permanent. Second, seeking possessions is not the goal for having one find happiness. Third, there is no eternal soul, and your quote 'self" is just a collection of your changing characteristics. Next, Noble Truths. One, there is a lot of suffering in life. Two, the cause of the suffering is greed. Three, there can be an end to suffering. Four, the way to its end is to follow the Middle Path." Zachary had all this memorized but now focused his eyes on Fila's to be sure she was catching it. She was.

"Okay, the eight Guides. Now I'm really testing my memory. Okay, one. You have to have the proper understanding of all the Truths, the Universal and the Noble. Two, you have to have the right values, like you can't be selfish. Three, you should speak properly, like not tell lies or be abusive. Four, you have to do right, like not harm others. Five, do the right work, be useful. Six, give the right effort, be helpful. Let's see, seven … have the right awareness, be mindful…. Hmmm… eight, okay, have a calm mind, meditate. Wow! I did it."

"Bravo, Zach. That was great, I wish everyone in the world could adopt those eight Guides. That would mean peace." Fila sat up and reached her hand to Zachary's cheek, giving it a slow, warm touch.

Zachary could feel his heart begin to pound. That was the first time Fila had ever touched him. He took a deep breath as her hand withdrew, and he struggled to continue. "I agree. I like that too, but there is more to the story. The serious Buddha followers really got into meditation as an essential practice, a path to what they call 'nirvana', freedom from needless suffering…. Buddhism later spread east beyond India, into Asia, Japan, and today there are some five hundred million followers. They eventually expanded beyond the Eight Guides and added five daily guidelines, or Precepts, to follow. Some seem the same as the Guides. I remember them, too. Don't harm or kill living things, don't take things unless freely given to you, lead a decent life, don't speak unkindly or tell lies, and don't abuse drugs or alcohol. That's it!"

"Wow, let me absorb all that. Can we finish up with Hinduism another time? I'm excited now. Let's walk, dear Zach."

Pumped, Zachary reached down, grasped Fila's arm and pulled her abruptly up to her feet. "Lets' go, ready!" he exclaimed, looking directly into her bright green eyes. He felt proud that he had explained Buddhism so simply and clearly to her, and that it obviously had hit a tender spot within her, but he couldn't quite explain to himself why he felt so warm over his whole body at this moment.

Eleven

There had been no teaching done at the National University after 9/11/21. The faculty, lead by Michael, had all been fully consumed in helping solve the problems of water and food distribution, helping medical facilities to stay operational, and assisting electric utilities in regaining adequate electricity generation. Importation of food and water containers and their broad distribution by the trucking industry had certainly paid off. Quickly replenishing overwhelmed medical facilities with supplies and their emergency generators was a high priority. The biggest problem with restoring the national electric grid was the shortage of backup transformers to replace those many burned out by the strong electromagnetic pulse that had run through them. Despite many spotty improvements, Michael and his teams working with the electric industry still faced huge hurdles in restoring full capacity by the summer of 2023. Fortunately, with the Ebola virus dying off quickly the number one problem for Americans, who were no longer dominated by a farm society, was the daily need for food and water for every citizen, especially within the nation's large city populations.

Even with his long work days in Denver and frequent trips to Washington to consult with the federal government, which had fully relocated there, the late evenings found Michael continuing to focus his mind on that beautiful, mysterious woman who escaped his apartment and perhaps was the one seen by that gas station attendant as she walked through Glenwood Springs and towards the Roaring Fork Valley. He finally had in his possession the written and signed pardon granted to her by President Graham, by reason that the young Marine she had shot in the leg had fully recovered. Furthermore, subsequent to that shooting, the young Afghan woman, Fila, had redeemed herself by saving the day with Michael against the Ebola virus, that critical third day after the 9/11 attack.

Despite pleas from Rose for Michael to relax a little with her and little Alex on Sundays, he kept himself busy with work. At least that effort was in the couple's apartment and not in the university office. Finally, on one beautiful early August morning, Michael looked up from his breakfast reading in their apartment and announced to Rose: "Let's the three of us take a drive up to the mountains. There are now enough recharge stations open to get us to Aspen and back."

"Come on. Seriously, Aspen. That would mean getting home after dark tonight," Rose countered.

"No problem. Not dark til near nine. It's a beautiful day, and we do need a break. Let's pack some snacks. I'll get Alex dressed and …"

"Michael, you are still looking for Fila, aren't you?"

"Well, yes in a way. We have her pardon to give her, and you know my dearest, you are keen to find her too. We have so many more questions to ask her," Michael answered breaking a slight smile but looking down.

"Okay, okay, so we'll go," Rose replied without a smile.

It was approaching noon when Michael drove the Volt into the gas station at Glenwood Springs. Alex had fallen asleep in his rear car seat during the three-hour drive up into the heart of the Rockies. Rose was curious why Michael parked and exited the car so quickly, then remembered his story that a car attendant here thought he had seen a young woman of Fila's description passing through shortly after she had escaped their apartment, almost two years ago.

Feeling immediate relief, there inside the station Michael found himself face to face with the same young man he had spoken with before. "Hello, there. You might remember some time back I stopped here looking for a young lady friend who had gotten disoriented after the 9/11 chaos. She seemed to be roaming in the mountains, lost, and…"

"Sure, I remember. Yeah, I found her sometime ago. Like you, I thought she might need help, but she seemed okay." The response from the attendant, John Striver, was tart, with his head looking down as he spoke.

Michael temporarily froze, like he could not believe what he was hearing but then felt a sense of joy.

"Oh, that's great! … Gee, I thought you might contact me, if you remember I gave you my…"

"Yeah, that's right. Sorry," said John still looking down at some papers he was shuffling as he maintained his position behind the counter. He did not seem the least bit interested in pursuing Michael's inquiries any further.

Michael paused, then persisted, excitedly. "Okay, just one more minute of your time. You had told me she was headed towards Independence Pass. Where did you find her?"

John continued his ploy of looking busy even though there were no customers in sight.

"Please. She is a foreigner and she may still need help," Michael pleaded.

"Yeah, listen, if I remember, I spotted a girl who looked as you described walking along some road, I don't remember, in Basalt ... up the valley. She looked okay to me. Maybe that was the one you are looking for."

"Basalt, okay, thanks. We'll drive up. Please, this time, if we don't find her and you see her again, here is my card with my name and mobile number. Please call me."

John finally looked up and nodded, silent. As Michael said "thanks", left the station, got into the car and pulled out, John's wide eyes followed him with a long, cold stare.

———————•●•———————

After a half hour's drive up the Roaring Fork Valley on Highway 82, Michael spotted the signs for El Jebel and Basalt while Rose was peering at a map of the area. "Turn right here at this light. It goes into an area called the Willits Town Center. It's the beginning of Basalt."

"Looks like all new stores," Michael offered as he drove through, up and down each street, staring at every visible person.

"Michael, we are fairly intelligent people. This is ridiculous. We have one chance in a million of spotting her walking these little streets right at this time, and who knows, she now could be anywhere in this valley two years later, or not here at all." Rose's tone of voice was one of simple exasperation, but little could she fathom what was in Michael's heart if not his brain.

"Okay, right, but it's our only lead right now," Michael quietly replied. "Let me just stop in that Whole Foods store right there. They're open and everyone shops for whatever food is available. I'll ask about her."

Minutes later, "well?" Rose inquired.

"Mostly white people around here. The manager said she has never noticed a tan faced young woman with green eyes," Michael replied. "Let's go. There must be an old town." Michael resumed driving along each road to the last, Willits Lane, which returned to Highway 82 right at a traffic light at Two Rivers Road on the other side. Continuing across, there was no one walking along the roadside until the next mile entering downtown Basalt. Only a few roads there in this small town, and Michael slowly drove along them all -- carefully looking at each person encountered. Then approaching the end of Midland Avenue, he spotted an open front door to Saint Vincent's Catholic Church. "The church!" he exclaimed. "They would know everybody in this town." Quickly parking the car, Michael leaned toward Rose. "Get Alex out, we going in."

The last Sunday Mass had ended. The church was nearly empty of people inside. Along side an aisle near the front, Michael spotted an elderly woman reshuffling prayer books. Rushing up, with Rose and little Alex behind, Michael voiced out, "Excuse me, ma'am, we missed the services. We're looking for a friend, a tan skinned young woman, very pretty with bright green eyes. A foreigner with an accent. Her name is Fila. Have you..."

"Oh, you mean Mary," the older woman blurted out, straightening up and smiling broadly. Not Fila ... Mary. A delight, very pretty, she helps here a lot. She..."

Now for the first time Rose perked up, interrupting, "You mean she is fairly young, about thirty years old, has a foreign accent, bronze skin, attractive, very green eyes, medium build, nice figure?"

"Yes, yes, that's her. She came here from a deserted family situation right after 9/11 and helps out here several times week.

Mary. Yes, somewhere abroad, I think raised in the Caribbean. She was just here for our Mass. A good Catholic, you know. Now everyone is gone for the day."

Michael thought quickly, *a good Catholic … Mary. Maybe her guise to remain undetected as a 9/11 assassin.* "Oh, that's great. We are friends, I'm Michael, my wife Rose, and our son, Alex. We have not seen her since 9/11. So much turmoil you know. Can you tell us where she is? Where she lives?"

"Oh, certainly. She has been taken in by our dear friend of the parish, Colleen Gelayes. They live down by the end of Two Rivers Road. I don't know the address, but down near where the road meets the highway at the light."

The faces of Michael and Rose both seemed to light up. Michael could not hide his excitement. "Gosh, we cannot thank you enough. That's so great. We'll just head down that way now. You've been so helpful."

"Yes, yes, thank you so very much," said Rose. "And your name?"

"Hilda." Her voice was barely audible as Michael scooped up Alex and with Rose right behind, they were out the door in a flash.

———————◆•◆———————

Using the street map that Rose had picked up at a service station after leaving Glenwood Springs and with Michael at the wheel, the Volt sprinted down Two Rivers Road until the traffic light at the Highway 82 intersection could be seen. There were no homes on Two Rivers Road but Michael could see a turnoff going up hill just before the intersection. Turning right he almost immediately came to a right/left choice. Turning right, he drove past five substantial homes on a street named Silverado Drive to a cul-de-sac and turned around as no one was in sight. The other side was named Hillcrest Drive, and the road appeared to zig zag uphill with a few nice looking homes on both sides. Appearing quite quickly on that uphill route, a dead end branch veered off to the left with one home at the end. Continuing turning uphill to the right a short ways, he sighted a man appearing to be working in his garden. Michael stopped the car, and the three quickly exited and approached the lone figure, a middle aged man in work clothes appearing to be pulling weeds from a garden of tomatoes.

"Excuse me, sir", Michael spoke up forcibly. "Sorry to interrupt your work, but we were told an old friend might be residing nearby. We just wanted to say hello to her, a young foreign girl, tan skin, green eyes…."

A pause as the gentleman eyed the three. "You mean Mary. Of course, everyone wants to say hello to her. Been here since the 9/11 chaos. A real nice person -- helps everyone out. We all appreciate what that whole Gelayes family does for all of us. Especially all the game and fish and water they bring to everyone in need here. So, you want to see her?"

"Yes, yes, we surely do. We've missed her. We lost track for a while after we all got confused in the 9/11 mess. Can you tell us which home, you say the Gelayes family's?" Rose asked excitedly.

"Sure. Right there. Right up the drive before my house."

———————●●———————

Michael knocked repeatedly on the door, looked in the windows, walked around the house. "Michael, stop it. It's obvious no one's home. We've been here an hour. They must have a Sunday afternoon outing. We have to get going back. I don't want you driving in the dark, and Alex is getting fussy. And you know, my boy, you've been getting such little sleep."

"Okay, Rose. Let's go. I have to be in early tomorrow. At least we know where she is. Finally, we've found her. This 'Mary' has to be Fila. Let's not leave a note – don't want to possibly frighten her."

The long road home, with an hour stop for battery recharging and a snack, was quiet, almost silent, but with obvious gratification showing on the two faces of Michael and Rose -- the whereabouts of long, lost Fila, the terrorist then heroic and pardoned, had been discovered.

Twelve

"Look at those beautiful golden leaves," pronounced Zachary. "Makes life worth living." It was Sunday September 10th 2023. The spectacular Aspen trees were beginning to appear in their full autumn glory. Zachary was walking Fila back home down Two Rivers Road after finishing clean up chores upon completion of church services in Old Town Basalt. It was at a point in the road where Mt. Sopris comes into clear view. Fila paused and stared at the twin peaked, free-standing mountain. "Always awesome, huh?" Zachary added.

"Zach, would you mind if we crossed the highway and strolled along the back trail a bit towards that mountain? You know tomorrow is a date in my life I wish I could forget. But of course, I can't." Sensing Fila's somber tone, Zachary was quick to respond. "Right, it's two years now, but sure - it's Sunday afternoon, we have lots of time today. Let's go."

Crossing Highway 82 at the traffic light leads into Willets Lane, which leads up to the newer commercial area of Basalt. But following alongside 82 a very short walk back towards older Basalt leads to a narrow road named Sopris Creek Road, which in a short way divides into two – East and West. Taking the West fork leads one quickly to a spectacular view of Mt. Sopris, less than five miles away to its peaks as the crow fly's.

"Spectacular! Thanks Zach. There is something magical about that mountain. I don't know … maybe…."

"Remember I said we would climb it, but so far not enough time. Someday. But you know, it's two years here now Fila. I know you have always been troubled by what brought you here … what you and your former so-called friends tried to do, but that's all over now. You're starting a new life. My family, my family … I, we, we all love you. You are welcome to be with us." Zachary's heart strings were pouring out. "We have been studying all these religions together. You are getting answers…"

"I know, Zach, and thank you, but…."

"But what?" Zachary pleaded as they continued their stroll through the fields, with visions of beauty surrounding all around them.

"Okay, yes, I'm understanding all these different creeds and ways of worship and paths to righteous living but so many unanswered questions. I need more."

"More, Fila, more? Why not just grab onto one and live it? You have repented. You are forgiven. What is it that you really want?"

A brief silence ensued as they continued to walk slowly on. Then Fila stopped and put her hand on Zachary's forearm, stopping him and looking him squarely in his longing eyes.

"I want to know everything about our human nature. I want to know why humans behave both with love and with hate, good deeds and bad deeds, compassion and violence … and then Zach I want to find answers. The history books I have read – wars, wars, fighting always, violence, and more violence. I know cooperation and working together has advanced man in so many ways but still the violence -- it goes on and on. I want to help find a way to stop the madness that I have seen almost my whole life. I want to see it stopped." As she turned her face and gazed at the mountain, tears came to her eyes.

Zachary stared at her in amazement. *Where did this come from?*

She continued talking on, dropping her hand from his arm and renewing her slow walk. He followed her, listening closely.

"Zach, while you have been working hard with your dad, and when I was not doing my chores or helping your mom at church, I have been to the library many, many times myself. In addition to the religions we have been studying together, which as you know some are closer to philosophy, the study of all things as to how everything is what it is, or how it should be. And, I have been reading up on the great philosophers, scientists, and those who have made a great impact on societies in the past. Now I am far from drawing any conclusions, but I will get there."

Zachary could in no way now focus on the surrounding view nor the scene of Sopris getting closer. He was totally fixated on this beautiful woman now letting it all out. Any past dreams of her sex appeal were dissipated. It was like listening to the best professor he ever had in college lecture halls.

"There are some things I can tell you now. I've learned so much about the evolution of the planet, from creation to microscopic bacterial life to the huge dinosaurs, to their getting wiped out sixty five million years ago from the implosion of a big meteor hitting Mexico, to the survival of little tiny mammals, to our upright species in Africa, homo erectus, to our big brain, homo sapiens, with our large frontal cortex developing some three hundred thousand years ago – all those centuries of evolution of our DNA genetic code giving us certain basic behavior patterns – to the agricultural revolution in the middle east just ten thousand years ago, the start of our writing, our history books, giving rise to towns, language, and culture, to the great religions ... can you believe, all those major religions we have today started in only a period of over about three thousand years in this long time frame of human development.... Why is that, Zach? Is it because this new philosophical thinking man a couple thousand years ago realized that he was so fundamentally and inherently disorderly that he needed a strong all encompassing code to live by to bring order to society, to put an end to superstitious pagan gods ... or what?" Fila paused and looked over to Zachary's incredulous appearing face. "I'm sorry, dear friend. I'm carrying on well before I should and..."

"No, no," Zachary interrupted. " I am amazed and gratified that I am so fortunate to have you as dear friend. I want you to continue on. Follow your dream. You have more courage and wisdom than anyone I could ever hope to meet. Please, continue. I know now, you want the answers and then you want the solutions."

"Well, okay, I think that's enough for now, I thank you for listening to this confused, uncertain, ranting gal you've teamed up with. You have to know how much I respect you, dear Zach." She smiled at him warmly and then turned to have a full view of Sopris right in front of her. "Some day, I'll climb to the top of that mountain ... and I'll have the answers, and then I'll get the solutions. Now, lets head home. Your mom has a great Sunday dinner planned, and I'm going to help her."

Thirteen

Saturday evening, October 21, 2023.

"Rose, it has to be tomorrow. Alexis's formal election 2024 campaign for president kicks off in a couple of weeks, and you know where she wants me. I just have to get up to Basalt and talk to Fila. I can find her at the church we found." A long silence ensued.

Michael, sitting at the kitchen table, looked down. Rose got up and stood over his bowed head, speaking in a very stern manner. "Look, you know how I feel about this, Michael. She has been pardoned by Alexis, the President of the United States, despite the military's balking because of the wounded Marine as well as the whole 9/11 attack. There is no reason you have to talk to her despite your telling me you want to learn more about their attack on us. It's over. It's been two years. It's been slow progress but steady. You have been instrumental in bringing the United States back towards normal, but you know there is still much more to be done. Why can't you leave this alone?"

Rose stood and stared at him a few moments longer, Michael not responding, not moving. She finally spoke, more softly now. "Okay … I have to take Alex to a meeting tomorrow morning with the young mother's group. Do as you want. Please be home for dinner."

━━━━●•●━━━━

On Sunday morning, Michael was out of bed before dawn. He dressed without waking Rose or little Alex and was in his fully charged Volt by 6 a.m. He was through the Eisenhower Tunnel at the Continental Divide by 8 and near Old Basalt by 10. He stopped at the red light at Highway 82 and Two Rivers Road. He remembered the house shown to him where it was thought Fila now lived. On green he turned his car left and another left. He could see the home but no one was in sight. His plan was to get to the church he had first learned that she assisted in Sunday morning services. He remembered the older woman named Hilda who said a pretty young woman who fit the description of Fila, "Mary" she called her, was there often. He remembered it was Saint Vincent's Catholic Church near the end of Midland Avenue in the old town. Turning the Volt around and back to Two Rivers Road, tracking the mile up to the old town, Michael turned right on Midland Avenue, past a dozen stores left and right and there it was – a nice looking church with cars completely filling the parking spots in front. He drove a little ways up the street until he found an empty space. He hurriedly found his way to the front door and upon entering stood frozen looking at a congregation filling each and every sitting space.

Reclining against the back wall as Holy Communion was about to begin, Michael spotted her. He stood straight up abruptly. There she was standing in the front near the altar holding a red wine cup for the communion takers who were beginning to quietly stand up and file to the front. He could hear faint organ music in the background but quickly lost sight of her beyond the standing and slow moving parishioners. In a few minutes everyone had returned to one's seats. A priest was moving forward from the altar to speak while Michael's eyes were fixed on Fila, returning the wine cup to a location at the rear of the altar. Her golden complexion and dark hair looked the same but she was too far away to clearly discern her features. *That's her. That is definitely she. Mary, Mary … that's Fila for sure. Finally.*

His eyes fixed upon her return to a seat near the front of the congregation.

The Mass ended. The organ music became louder. People stood up and began quietly filing out. Michael's eyes remained fixated on Fila standing up and beginning to chat with a middle-aged couple and perhaps their two teenagers. He moved quickly towards them. "Mary," he exclaimed quite dramatically. "I'm so glad I bumped into you here. What a surprise."

Fila turned towards him, and her facial expression turned to one in shock. Her mouth dropped, and her eyes opened wide in disbelief. A brief pause as they stared at each other, Michael with a slight smile, then. "Michael! Is that you? I, I …"

Michael was prepared. "Yes, Mary. I was returning from Aspen and thought I would drop by for a little religion on my way back to Denver. How have you been? You look well. And your friends here?" Michael turned and looked smilingly at Grace, Zachary, and Colleen. "You're friends of Mary's?"

Colleen sensed Michael's warmth and quickly responded. "Yes, yes we are. Right after our national tragedy two years ago, in God's good Grace, Mary came to us and has been living and flourishing with us and our community ever since. This is my son Zachary and daughter Grace. And you…"

Michael was quick to chime in without answering Colleen's question. "Well good, nice to meet you all," as all nodded and looked a little bit taken back. Michael did not allow the conversation to go on. "I have to run, but do you all mind if I just catch up with Mary a moment. We had been concerned about her but so glad you folks have helped her sort it all out." Without a pause for a retort, Michael softly took Fila's arm and began to lead the two of them across the church to the other side. "So pleased to have met you all," he said on the way. The family of four stared at him a moment and then with Colleen in the lead began moving towards the open front doors of the church, turning their heads back twice as they walked to see Michael and "Mary" sitting down in the first row.

By this time, Fila had regained her composure. They stared deeply into each other's eyes, barely twelve inches apart, searching for meaning, for compassion. "Michael, oh Michael. What are you doing here? How did you find me? Are you here to take me back? I am good here. I am helping them. I never want to hurt anybody again. I …"

"Stop, stop, dear Fila. I am not here to take you back. Your wounded Marine has recovered just fine. Yes, our military brass was a little upset with you for aligning yourself with foreign terrorists, attempting to destroy our country, and shooting and wounding a United States soldier, but they were overruled by our president, Alexis Graham. As president, she has the constitutional right to pardon and she has formally pardoned you of any all misdeeds. She knows the full story that we might all be quite gone now if you hadn't realized your mistaken beliefs and misguided mission and not saved us that third day in the lab. Here, your written pardon is in this envelope. Hold onto it.

"Hey, I even forgive you for conking me hard on the head with the butt of that rifle you were sporting," he said with a chuckle. "You are now a free person, Fila." Michael smiled warmly at that, reached his hand out and hugged her shoulder. Fila closed her eyes, a tear showing and dropping from each.

"My purpose of finding you and coming here today is not only to make sure you are okay and to hand you your pardon, but to also tell you I want to communicate with you. I have been and will continue to try to be of service to my country, but I also want to better understand how your comrades were able to pull off such as major, surprise attack on us. I know it's painful for you to bring up the subject, but I'm afraid in this age of weapons of mass destruction - chemical, biological and nuclear - that it is no longer just a major power able to commit such horror, but also smaller, rogue nations or even groups of terrorists."

Regaining her composure, Fila responded. "Oh Michael, I am so sorry. I sounded so selfish. Yes, I will help you in any way I can … just so you can leave me here. These kind people have become my loving family. It's all I have."

"Absolutely. I understand. But I want you to know you have **me** too. I remain your friend, as we tried to be in my apartment two years ago. I understand your leaving then without a trace. That's all in the past. Let's make a new beginning. I planned for this when I knew I would find you." Reaching into his jacket pocket, "Here, this is the most powerful satellite cell phone in the world, and here is the charger. I want you to text message this number written on the back when you are alone for awhile each week and give me three times that I can call you when you are completely alone for at least ten minutes. Then I'll call you so we can talk business… and Fila dear, please, at any time you want to talk to me for any reason right away, please call and hopefully I'll be available." He gave her shoulder another gentle hug.

With no one in the church now except Hilda in the back pew bent over shuffling books around their holders, Fila took both her arms and pulled Michael closer, hugged Michael warmly, cheek to cheek, tears openly flowing. "I want answers too Michael, I want answers too," she sobbed softly.

Fourteen

As winter approached in late November 2023, the shortened daylight hours and extended dark period was the best period in recent Basalt life, the season's best well-being the last three approaching winters. Damaged electric transformers throughout Colorado were almost fully replaced. Pumps needed for drawing water up from wells and pumps to push waste to septic tanks were almost fully working again. Food markets were at least half stocked again, meaning the Basalt locals did not have to rely as much on persons such as George and Zachary spending so much time on efforts fishing and hunting. The two continued their efforts primarily for their own family instead of so much for their whole community. They were able to spend more time at home with the coming snowstorms.

"Mom, Dad, I checked it out. By late next summer I may be able to attend a graduate school that I read may open again. I sure would like to attend a university in Denver where I can get a master's degree in religion," Zachary stated at dinner one evening as the five were finishing up. Colleen did not look up or reply but extended a warm smile towards him. Grace sat quietly with a look of bewilderment. Fila was taken back with a look of surprise. With all their many talks and library research projects together, she could not imagine a life without her dear

Zach. She felt so emotionally attached to him. He was so kind, starting that first night when he opened the front door and took her in. Too young to be physically attached to him but to her old enough to be overflowing with his growing wisdom that she prized. A true friend, but could he really leave his family, and me? *Maybe he wants to test his parent's thoughts about this. He knows how much they have depended on him through the many crisis months.*

"Zachary! What are you talking about? We are not yet in a stable situation. We need your help around here. I don't know when I can make a stable living again let alone afford graduate tuition for you. And besides, you have already learned enough about religion – where has your God been in all this mess?" George looked right at Zachary with a stern face.

"George, stop it! We agreed long ago our differences on matters of faith are not to be discussed." Colleen was clearly showing her displeasure at her husband's harsh remarks. "When things return to normal, Zachary is free to lead his own life, his own destiny, but for now Zach, let's just concentrate on our welfare here and on helping our Basalt community. No more talk about leaving." Zachary was quiet. He knew his family's welfare came first. Fila felt herself smiling, hopefully no one noticing.

The winter days though December and early 2024 experienced harsh winds and an unusually cold season, with more than the average winter snowfall. The five kept themselves plenty busy with Grace spending time with her mother in home schooling, George and Zach fishing and hunting as the weather allowed, and Colleen helping out with the older parishioners at Saint Vincent's. Fila had her share of household duties as well as helping Colleen with matters at church, but during her free time she managed to walk the mile to the Basalt Free Library.

She also learned that come springtime she would be able to hitch a ride twenty miles to the much larger Aspen Free Library.

On many occasions before leaving the Basalt library when Zachary was not with her, she spent time messaging and calling Michael. From his training as an engineer, he methodically drew from her everything she knew about Dire, the island in the Indian Ocean now apparently destroyed by Chinese nuclear weapons. How she got there; for what reason; who was in charge; what their purpose was, their motive; how did they obtain a nuclear bomb; where and how was it launched to be exploded two hundred miles above Kansas; how did they hire the American scientist Jonathan Dean who managed to genetically make the Ebola virus contagious airborne; how did they obtain all the personnel who spread the virus through the United States; how did they convince you Fila that your vaccine shot would give you immunity when it was really worthless; how was all this financed; exactly why they thought they needed assassins on top of their two weapon attack on 9/11; how did they and with what methods convince her to join them after she went to Dire to find peace from the turmoil in Afghanistan; how did she train. His questions were endless and he wanted detailed answers. But he always ended their conversations wanting to know how she was, how she was getting along. Did she ever think of returning?

———————•◆•———————

Winter of 2024 in Basalt passed uneventful. George and Zachary pursued their fishing and hunting excursions even though more and more foodstuffs were appearing at the local food markets. Colleen with Fila's assistance made sure the daily breakfasts and dinners were wholesome, the house and clothing were clean and in good repair, the wood stove was fully functioning, St. Vincent's was getting its needed help, and Grace was studious in her home schooling. Fila stayed in touch with the ever-busy Michael on the satellite cell phone he had provided her. Their conversations always ended on a personal note expressing warm wishes for good health.

But Spring came with the kind of experiences Fila had thought about but prayed would never occur. It had been two and a half years as "Mary" living with the Gelayes family, becoming a valuable part of the community assisting those in need of assistance, and mysteriously disappearing into the town library for hours and hours "studying" they said, but no one but Zachary Gelayes knew what. From the first hour, George had always seemed to be looking beyond her outward presence, sort of like he was undressing her. She could sense his peering deep into her eyes, studying her silky long black hair, and most sensuous her well-curved body, particularly when she was scantily dressed in and out of the bathroom, or a warm summer day outside. For George, having daily daydreams of leading her to his bed, removing her clothes, and having ecstatic sex always conflicted with his after thoughts that this Afghan girl was a curse that unexpectedly had come upon his door uninvited.

George's anticipated dream scene happened on a Sunday morning when Fila was sent back home to retrieve Colleen's personal Bible that she had forgotten to take to church with her. Fila was wearing a short black skirt, a light pink blouse tightly fitted and a black sweater loosely around her shoulders, an outfit that Colleen had recently gifted her as an Easter present. Unintended in Colleen's mind, but Fila looked very sexy in that outfit. George was standing in the master bedroom half dressed when Fila suddenly appeared to retrieve Colleen's Bible on her night table. Her face suddenly turned to a started look as she was obviously surprised to see George in the bedroom this late in the morning.

"Oh, sorry George. Colleen forgot her Bible and sent me back for it. She said it was on her night table. I …"

"No, no, come in," a surprised but pleased looking George quickly stated, standing on the other side of the bed next to Colleen's night table. "Here, it's over here. Come around." His face turned to a smile. Not a sound could be heard. But when Fila quickly passed from inside the doorway to the other side of the bed, George remained still, blocking her passage to the Bible on the table. His eyes widened, staring intently at her up and down. She had no choice but to pause her progress, standing a foot away from him. He spoke rapidly. "Look, Fila, you have been with us a long time. You are now part of our family. I think it's time …" She suddenly felt her fear. She had seen this look before. He reached out towards her and stretched his strong arms around her back and shoulders but not getting a welcoming response, thrust her down onto the bed, maneuvering his half nude body on top of hers. She felt his weight, his hot breath, as he blurted out: "Please, please, don't resist young lady, his hands now probing for her breasts. Let's make this consensual." He was trying desperately to control any feeling of rage in response to her resistance. He wanted her consent.

Fila finally found her voice after the initial shock, trying to push his heavy weight up. "George! No, no, this is not what we are supposed to do. You have a beautiful, loving wife. I am not going to be your mistress. Get off me!" But George did not budge, did not speak, pausing in his physical effort to seduce, seemingly searching to find the answer to his next move. Feeling his heavy weight, Fila stopped her resistance, waiting for his response to her plea, but in her mind there was no way she was going to allow herself to be raped. She was well trained in the martial arts and knew where to strike in a strategic location.

George finally relented and rolled off her. If not in his actions, at least in his mind he wanted this encounter to be consensual. He somehow, to his own surprise, came to his senses despite the strong masculine emotions he was feeling. On his back now on the bed, he stared up at the ceiling. His voice was strong and clear. "We'll see. We'll see. You're not going it have it that easy, our mystery woman of Asia."

Fila quickly composed herself, raised her body hurriedly from the bed, reached for and grabbed Colleen's Bible in her hand, and as she scurried out of the room, she could hear him continue his verbal rant.

"We saved her, we sheltered her, our house girl. We disguised her -- our virgin Mary. Ha!"

———•———

George Gelayes was not the only one beginning to make Fila feel uncomfortable. John Striver could not get this beautiful stranger out of his mind either. He found himself in almost daily imaginations of his making love to her. He had finally located her in his drive through Basalt. It seemed a very long time ago; it was time to go back. He had hoped that the guy named Michael Reynolds had never found her. He was bored working at his father's service station in Glenwood Springs, and he was finding no satisfaction with any of the local girls not yet married.

In his idle time, he enjoyed hunting for small game -- rabbits, squirrels, and the like. He didn't seem interested in big game even while meat was scarce the last few years, and he was never interested in a hunting rifle like his dad's. He had researched the best revolvers to use for small game and for target shooting, and after reviewing varieties from Smith &Weston, Glock, Magnum, Springfield, and Browning, he bought himself a .22 Ruger MK III. Its long barrel helped the pistol produce great accuracy upon firing.

John's dad found his son rather aimless and unambitious, somewhat a loner even though the folks of local communities had pulled together after the 9/11 crisis. To get his son out more, he was finally able to help him finance and purchase a seven year old hybrid SUV. John kept his new pistol in the unlocked glove compartment for convenience as he began to visit the target range more and more frequently as the snows melted from the winter of 2024.

It seemed almost every other day that John would take a quick ride up to Basalt to hopefully catch another glimpse of the mysterious woman who the stranger named Michael Reynolds said had been lost, the one who wanted directions to Independence, the one who returned his stare as he passed her on Two Rivers Road. On his trip Sunday, July 14, 2024, he was in luck. Turning left at the traffic light onto Two Rivers Rd. off Highway 82, no one was in sight. He proceeded the mile up Two Rivers Rd. sighting no one, so he continued on into Old Town Basalt and up Midland Avenue past the shops and restaurants again seeing no one, and about to turn around when all at once a crowd began pouring out of a church. As one car pulled out directly in front of the church, John parked his vehicle facing the building and stared at every single individual coming past. No beautiful young woman. The crowd was gone, but wait. A girl was bending down outside the open church door removing a doorstop and pulling the door closed. He caught her face. *Jesus, that's her!*

Only a quick glimpse, but he was sure she was the one he had been searching for. To him it then seemed that he was waiting an eternity, but soon coming out the door there appeared that same three again -- a middle-aged woman, a teenage girl, and **her**. His mind was racing, his heart pounding, and without any premeditation, he blurted out his window as they passed by: "Need a ride down Two Rivers, ladies? I'm headed that way."

Stopping to identify the voice of this kind offer, the three looked intently at the figure behind the wheel. Colleen was quick to react: "Oh, no thank you, young man. Very kind but we have stops to make," with a strong voice and then softly turning to Grace and Fila: "Come along, across the street into Skip's Market. Something I don't like about that guy's stares."

John lost sight of them as they hurried behind his vehicle and across the street. They disappeared. He backed out of his parking spot and slowly drove down the street. No sign of them. He was puzzled. He thought he was being polite. *Why would they hurry away from me? For some reason, maybe they have been taught not to talk to strangers.* After several turns up and back on Midland Avenue, John finally drove slowly back down Two Rivers Road to Highway 82 without spying anyone like the three women. He was beginning to feel enraged as he drove back to Glenwood Springs.

———————◆•◆———————

Breakfast at home now was quite uncomfortable for Fila as she could sense George's frequent glances, but she hurried things along, barely sitting down, keeping the pancakes or eggs or cereal items moving along for George, Zachary and Grace, assisting Colleen with the dishes, glasses, and silverware. After cleaning up, everyone moved ahead quickly to their daily duties and chores. But dinner was different. The family custom was to let the women prepare the meal, set the table, and they all would sit down together. Colleen would recite a prayer of thanks, and all would commence eating, together. No rush. Fila had always felt uncomfortable with George's stares, but now it was overbearing. *Is it because he still thinks I'm a terrorist and doesn't trust me? Or is that man still trying to make an advance towards me because he thinks I'm attractive? Or is it both? Or maybe he thinks hard sex on me would be a form of revenge.* After the Sunday bedroom incident, she now had a difficult time looking at him or speaking to him, even when he addressed her.

"George," Colleen began at the dinner table, "this morning after church we had a strange experience, again. The same young man a while back, sometime last year, drove past the three of us and gave us a long, cold stare, not like anyone we know or anyone appearing to be helpful, even though he offered us a ride home, but a look I took as possibly threatening, so the three of us diverted away and then hustled home, and he disappeared down 82. I told Grace never to get in a car with a strange man. But that same young man, there he was parked right outside St. Vincent's this morning, and like I said he offered to give us a ride down Two Rivers. He sounded I guess polite, but I don't know, something about him I didn't like, just don't trust strangers that don't look right. That long stare of his. So we disappeared quickly from his view and that's why we got home so late from church today."

"Hey, three good looking gals! A young dude trying to be nice to the girls, staring them up and down, and offering rides," Zachary interjected with a laugh, but knew that answer would not fly. No one else even smiled.

"You did the right thing, dear," George said with a tone of authority. "Don't trust men you don't know. We are a tight community here, one helping another, but be careful of strangers. Here, we all know who is who ... with certain exceptions." Fila could sense that last comment, a dart meant for her.

"You know, it seems I've seen that face before, somehow. Glenwood Springs? Listen, maybe it's me," Fila lamented. "I'm trouble. I don't belong here. Maybe he is after me. Maybe he suspects who I really am. I can go, I can go."

"What!" Colleen exclaimed. "No way, Fila. You are family now. You …"

"We love you, Fila, Mary! You can't leave us," Grace cut in excitedly.

George, with his authoritarian tone of voice ended it. "No more. No more talk about this. Calm down. Fila is going nowhere. The next time you see this creep, get me immediately, or if I'm not near get his license number. I'll take care of it."

But it soon became more complicated than that.

———•———

John Striver simply would not give up. He figured things out. This woman, this incredible young woman, was being sought after by a guy from Denver. He had said she's a lost friend, but what kind of a friend would she be by not returning to Denver as things began settling down after the 9/11 disaster. She was looking for Independence. Maybe she learned that place way up near Independence Pass by the Continental Divide was a far out mining settlement years ago, and what she **really** wanted was nothing other than to get lost. But the days of Independence, that very little silver mining tent town, were long gone. Maybe she then wandered back down and becoming tired and hungry, found this family in Basalt. That woman and her teenager walking with her – I bet she became a member of that family! Church and all. *Maybe, just maybe, that's who she really is,* he thought to himself.

By early August, John was making it a point to drive along Two Rivers Road, at varying times Monday, Wednesday, and Friday one week and again Tuesdays, Thursdays, and Saturdays the next week. He was determined, unrelenting, to find this woman, and maybe take her away. Fila was trying diligently to keep herself as busy as possible, avoiding as best she could George's continuing glances, and making sure she was never in the house alone with him. Zachary was using every free hour to join Fila at the library as she continued her searches into the major religions, into the great philosophies, and into the known sciences of the world – all part of her continuing search for the meaning of human life and why good and evil can exist side by side.

Grace had now become a real young lady, physically developed, attracting the teenage boys' full attention, hounding Fila every night at bedtime with her never ceasing questions about love and sex. Michael was as busy as ever with the nation's pressing business but always finding a moment to speak on the satellite phone with Fila weekly. She never mentioned to him George's advance upon her or that strange young man passing by.

———•———

On a late Saturday afternoon at the library, Fila suddenly grabbed her small handbag and quickly rose. "Oh, Zach, I don't know how it got this late. I have to get home and help your mom with dinner."

"Go, go, I'll catch up to you in a minute. I have to put all these books away."

Moments later, John Striver was just about to give up any hope of sighting the mysterious young woman on this day of searching. When he finally decided to head back home, his

SUV happened to be at the juncture of Two Rivers Road and Midland Avenue, the library close by on Midland across the Roaring Fork River. Then suddenly out of nowhere, it seemed, there she was! *Oh my God, that's her!* At 5 p.m. in early August it was still quite light out. A beautiful clear, warm, early evening. *Yeah, that's her for sure,* he thought, and *by herself,* walking quite rapidly off Midland and starting down Two Rivers Road. Feeling himself getting excited now, his heart beating wildly, he began to follow her, his vehicle passing her, and then slowing up abruptly just in front of her, momentarily stopping her progress. He jumped out as she began walking again around the vehicle, and then they met -- face to face. She stopped as he blocked her path. *Oh no,* she thought. "Hello, don't you remember me? … The service station in Glenwood Springs, you asking me the way to Independence … right after 9/11?" He spoke hurriedly, excitedly, but clearly, staring right into her eyes, closely, a foot away. Again, Fila could sense a restless male -- an uncomfortable feeling, but not one of helplessness. She had been trained.

A pause as they continued staring, and then Fila thinking, thinking, replied in deceit. She did not want to be identified as a runaway, and she also recognized this face as the same young man Colleen had had a strange sense about. "No, no. Not me. It has been years since I was in Glenwood Springs, and I know for sure -- not there around 9/11. Sorry, must have been someone else. I'm in a hurry, so … goodbye now." As she started to make her way around John and his large SUV, he put out his strong right arm and stopped her.

"Wait!" he shouted out firmly.

John had been a very strong football player in his high school days, and she could feel the strength in his one arm blocking her as he leaned it against her shoulders. There was virtually no room between his parked vehicle and a sharp drop off to her other side. She could feel her own heartbeats' rapid rise. Of course, she was no amateur in dealing with the martial arts, but refrained from attempting any physical action, and trying to act calm said to him quite sternly but politely, "Look young man, as I said, I am not that person you described. Please let me pass."

John was now more determined than ever. It had taken all this time to have her in front of him, alone. He was not going to give up now. "I think you're wrong; you were the one in trouble with the military weren't you? You've been hiding, right? Well, I'm saving you. You're good with me. It can be our secret. Listen, you're coming away with me, right now." He put his other arm around her waist and with both arms began pulling her towards the still open door of the SUV. He had both her arms pinned. She sensed his superior strength as tried getting her fingers pointed towards his eyes to attempt to puncture him. She could not reach her arms out from his strong embrace, but she was able to get her knee into a position to deliver a solid blow to her assailant's testicles. He fell back in pain and released her midsection but did manage to grab one of her ankles as she turned away to run. She tripped to the ground, and in an instant he was on top of her and gave her a hard, solid blow to the side of her head with his elbow knocking her dizzy, momentarily stunned. She felt the pain and struggled to move.

At that moment, a startled, bewildered Zachary was upon the scene, screaming "Fila, Fila, hey, what are you doing man?" He tried grabbing John from behind and pull him away from the fallen Fila, but in full adrenaline mode, John turned up and around and punched Zachary with all his force, square in the nose. With Fila on the ground dazed and Zachary on the ground holding his face in pain, a limping but determined John climbed into his vehicle and pulled out the Ruger from the glove compartment.

Back out to the ground, he screamed: "I'm taking you with me. Get up, get in," pointing the pistol at Fila, now trying to regain her footing.

"No way you are, don't be a fool. Put that gun away and get out of here," Zachary bravely retorted dropping his hands from his bleeding nose while struggling to get up.

The shot seemed incredibly loud in Fila's ears, still ringing from the side blow to her head. She first thought to run, maybe down to the river and hide from this maniac, but her compassionate instinct overruled again, just like she could not assassinate Rose Haines holding her baby on 9/11. She could not help herself. Her only thought was to go to her friend's aid. Instead of the choices of running to escape or confronting John head on, she instinctively lunged across and stretched her body over a fallen Zachary, now lying on his back and bleeding from the bullet wound high on his chest, just below his neck. She pressed the palm of her hand firmly over the spot of his shot wound, his shirt filling with blood. She had to stop the bleeding. Be damned what this crazy guy did next to her.

She barely noticed John running off in his SUV. Her thoughts were totally on not seeing this young man bleed to death. She thought *thank goodness* when she heard people approaching and one shouting out "call for an ambulance".

Meanwhile, John's first instinct had been to lift this girl up, force her into his SUV, and take off together, to continue the fight to win her over, with whatever means. But as just as quickly, his own fears took over. Complex emotions filled his brain, at first confusing him, but in his more rational mind he knew he had just done wrong. He knew he had committed a crime, maybe murder. His "fight or flight" instinct was to go to the latter -- get into his SUV and flee. As he did so, he could hear voices in the distance. *People must have heard the shot. No time for her now.*

———————•————————

There had been no direct witnesses to the shooting other than Fila. She gave a detailed description of the young man and his vehicle to police, but a month later there was still no sighting of either. The bullet had entered Zachary from his front, just below his clavicle, barely missing his heart, grazing his lungs, and settling into his third thoracic vertebrae. Compared to a hunting rifle bullet that would have produced shock waves and shattered and spread bone fragments, the smaller .22 inch diameter bullet spared his life but ended up shearing and partially tearing his third vertebrae. During the first few weeks after the shooting, Zachary was experiencing heart and lung problems but those symptoms were steadily declining. There was complete paralysis of the motor and nerve functions in his legs, bowels and bladder. He was to become a complete paraplegic, although some of the orthopedic doctors at Aspen Valley Hospital who treated him believed that after the initial spinal shock, lasting about two months, there would be some hope of partial sensation and leg movement recovery.

The glances at the Gelayes home took on a new look and tone. Young Grace could not come to a conclusion. She became quite quiet around Fila, their cozy bedtime chats now just a silent going to sleep routine. Colleen remained a strong believer in her faith. 'God works in mysterious ways', she had been taught. Her daily prayers were now completely dedicated to her son's recovery and possibly someday to Christian forgiveness of the shooter. Out loud at least, she never spoke words of blame addressed towards Fila. That was reserved to George. Gone now were his secret glances of hope for romantic interludes. More and more often as August ended and the days of autumn began, George's constant glances of scorn directed towards Fila worsened and were about to erupt into explosive words. Even though Fila had visited Zachary for hours on end in the hospital helping the nurses, endeavoring to comfort him, and even while after he had retuned home on a wheelchair, she had catered to his every need, the household mood was quiet and somber.

Finally, Fila felt compelled to speak out. "You don't have to say it, George. I'll say it for you. I'm 'trouble' who arrived on your doorstep. You didn't ask for it, you didn't want it. I was blessed by your family for giving me another chance in life. But I'm still 'evil arrived'. I have stayed the last month only so I could help out with Zach when you are all so busy. I have found a job and a room rental in Carbondale. I'll move there temporarily until I figure what's next in my life. I just want to say again I'm so sorry for what's happened, and, and … that I learned the meaning of true love having been with you all these last three years…. And one more thing, I have a very important friend in high circles in this country. We will find that guy, that guy that shot Zach. He will face justice for what he's done to him."

"And this time, there will be no begging for you to stay," George uttered in his usual stern voice, looking down, and for the first time not showering Fila with steady glances of any kind. Silence ensued again around the dinner table, Colleen and Grace both looking down, a tear falling from each of their eyes. Zachary in his nearby wheelchair seemingly lost for words, his face revealing nothing but a look of sadness.

PART 2

Fifteen

Carbondale is an artisan-oriented town just a few miles down Highway 82 from Basalt towards the direction of Glenwood Springs. It sits on the south bank of the Roaring Fork River at its confluence with the Crystal River. Route 133 comes off Highway 82, dissects the center of town, and following it south just six miles sits the impressive twin peaked Mt. Sopris, standing out majestically all by itself. The early settlers who came to the area traveled from Carbondale, Pennsylvania around 1880. They were farmers and ranchers, and during the silver days supplied potatoes to the miners in Aspen. Coal was actually discovered later in the Crystal River Valley, and mines there operated until the early 1990's. The town's population in the 1890 silver boom was only less than 200, but by 2021 almost 7000. The ski boom in Aspen starting in the 1960's caused real estate prices there to greatly escalate, providing Carbondale with an attraction to its location by reason of lower housing costs for Aspen workers.

One such Aspen worker was Lily Lamont, a 50 year-old very attractive woman still in excellent physical condition, except for an injured knee from a ski accident on one of Aspen Mountain's difficult Black Diamond trails. With most patient rooms holding two patients, Fila and Lily had become acquainted one morning while Fila was visiting the recuperating Zachary. Lily had stayed overnight after undergoing some minor surgical repair on her injured knee. Dropping by to check on Lily was Dr. Chris Stanford, a family doctor from the Carbondale Family Practice.

How quickly they all had hit it off. Lily had been looking for an apartment mate to help share the rent expense as she had an extra bedroom at her complex in Carbondale. It was an ideal location, on the top floor of a well-maintained, three-story brown brick building, the highest in town, at the corner of South 2nd and Main Street. Lily's corner apartment had an outdoor patio with a clear, direct view facing the ever-enticing Mt. Sopris. Meantime, Chris had been searching for an additional administrative assistant at his family medical practice location just a few blocks away from downtown. In almost no time, Lily had her roommate, Chris had his assistant, and Fila had a way to make her break from the agony she knew she was causing the Gelayes family in Basalt. She could still continue to visit Zachary and still continue her library research, including at the more expansive Pitkin County Library in Aspen. Her work schedule with Chris' medical practice was only three days a week on 12 hour shifts – enough income earned to pay her share of the rent, food, clothing and any bus transportation to Basalt or Aspen from Carbondale.

Through all these happenings, Fila still managed to call Michael every few weeks using the satellite phone he had given her. If he was busy when she called, he managed to call her back it seemed in no time. She managed a very comfortable relationship with her new roommate, Lily, but their conversations seemed very business like, mostly centered around the day's activities. After Zachary was sent home in a wheelchair from the Aspen Hospital and Fila's visits there ended, Lily was a little curious as to why Fila could spend so much time at the Aspen library after riding the bus up together from Carbondale and riding back together eight hours later, but she never probed into any detail. She seemed content that Fila was engaged in a "project". What to have for dinner together as her new apartment mate and friend was more important.

Two attractive women, living in the heart of this progressive town, but there was little talk of men. Lily had experienced a rough marriage, divorced after only two years and no children. She seemed to have no interest in meeting new single men in Aspen or Carbondale. Her handsome doctor friend, Chris, was happily married with two children. And she understood why her new apartment mate "Mary" seemed to have no interest in men after gone through the trauma of having her young friend Zachary shot by another man with the shooter still at large. The two women were getting along just fine without additional complications.

———————•————————

"Michael, I have gone over this so many times," Fila shut her eyes and grimaced holding the phone close to her ear. "Yes, yes, I did. As I told you, I described his looks and his SUV to the county police. Yes, it's the same guy you also met at the service station in Glenwood Springs…. Right, the police have visited the Gelayes at least three times now. They insist they have visited both the station and young man's home several times. His father insists his boy has disappeared, no sight of him, no word from him since the day of the shooting…. Okay, okay, I know you're trying to help and police forces have been overwhelmed since 9/11. Food and power have been all consuming, I understand, but Michael you do understand don't you that I can't sleep right at night. First, my horrible assault on

Rose and now almost losing this great kid. Zachary is a gem, a smart wonderful boy who has encouraged me so much in my quest for knowledge, and now he is a paraplegic, all because of me…. Thank you, Michael, yes, yes, I will keep my chin up. You know I can't do without your support…. No, you are so far away and so busy – you don't have to come. You know I'm not coming back to Denver. Yes, I'm all right. Yes, I will call you next week."

So, through the balance of 2024 and through the year 2025, this scenario continued to play out. Fila visiting Zach when no one else home. The two friends comforting each other in their mutual distress. Zach never once casting any blame on Fila. Fila feeling guilt but buoyed by Zach' s uplifting spirit. On Sundays, Fila occasionally going to Catholic Church masses in Basalt, "Mary" being greeted warmly by all, even including Colleen and Grace. Christian forgiveness and the knowledge that it was the still missing John Striver who was the one to blame for the shooting, not "Mary". Michael and Fila were speaking frequently on the phone, sharing their burdens, an ever- strengthening rapport. Fila's continuing bus rides to the Aspen library, spending long hours there in solitude, reading, studying, in deep thought. Lily and Fila getting along fine as apartment mates, scrupulously avoiding discussion of men despite their attractiveness and the attention given them when out in public. Fila working smoothly in Chris' medical offices three long days a week, and even getting some tips from Chris about what to read about brain problems as some of his patients had mental illness diagnoses. Fila, with ever an eye peering at the beauty of Mt. Sopris, through the changing seasons and through changes in light and weather, the sight always awesome.

In the early Spring of 2026, the magical sight and appeal of the twin peaked mountain became irresistible to Fila. She learned about the reputation for being a difficult climb to the top but far from overwhelming for a person in good shape. While the mountain still had quite a bit of snow on top, it could be time to at least make an initial climb to the base of the rocky, snow packed area. She just could no longer stay away from that mountain. A full climb could be achieved in the summer months of July or August.

Sixteen

Most mountains in the Rockies are linked. The famous Pikes Peak below Denver clearly stands out at the base of the mountain range, but as one travels high into the Continental Divide mountain area, the many linked peaks are outstandingly rugged and beautiful while the number attaining a height of 14,000 feet above sea level total some 58. The 12,953 foot elevated twin peaks of Mt. Sopris stand out as free standing, not linked in a chain, and one of the most photographed mountains in the Rockies. Approximately a little less than a mile stretch exists between the two peaks, only slightly below the summits, like a saddle. The mountain is part of the Elk Range in the White River National Forest, the peaks at approximately 6500 feet in altitude above the 6000 ft. elevation of Carbondale. The mountain is actually known as a growing rock glacier as more rocks near the top continue to become exposed. While the Elk Range mountains are primarily composed of red iron, the distinctive Mt. Sopris shows white rock near its summits, the white being quartz.

The climb up begins at a trailhead about a 4400 foot elevation to the top. An easy walk up from there extends back and forth some 3 miles to the Thomas Lakes, about a 1600 foot elevation gain, but the next zig-zag hike 3 miles up is a hiker's test, reaching the end of the tree line at about an 11,000 foot elevation. The final reach to the summit is the most difficult, steep and rocky. In summer, a good hiker can do the full 13 mile plus round trip from the trailhead in about 8 hours. In early spring 2026, Fila's hope was just to get to the snow line to get a feel for the full hike she was praying to make by August.

Meanwhile, she had a lot of work to do. In early May, she hitched a ride one Saturday morning to the trailhead and made the climb to just above the Thomas Lakes. Still in the tree line, she could not see too much from that location, but the experience invigorated her spirit all the more for the full climb by August. She was excited. She had to get all her notes in order, organize her thoughts, maybe unload her findings to dear friend Zach and maybe even the innocent, attentive Lily. She was beginning to understand mankind's historical and ongoing aggression and violence on the one hand and traits of cooperation and compassion on the other, but as of yet had no answers in coming up with solutions of how to slow the violence part. So many pray for world Peace, and so many preach Love as the answer, but now she knew there was so much more. So much more.

In the early morning of Saturday, June 6, she was siting comfortably on Lily's apartment deck working away on her findings and taking occasional glances at Sopris when the call on her phone showing it was Michael. It was usually her calling him first then waiting for his calling back as he was always so busy. *Fine, love to chat with him, especially to learn more about whether the nation's fortunes are continuing to improve.*

"Good morning out there. All is well?" he inquired routinely.

"Yes, quite fine here. A beautiful morning," she replied warmly. "And you?"

"As ever, we're full time working on improving people's lives and the economy. You know from what I've told you before, how few Americans have died from starvation and disease these last few years, but let's not dwell on that again. I guess we have done a pretty good job after that first horrible year after 9/11. Listen, I have different news."

"Okay, yes, what is it, Michael? Fila replied softly after trying to dismiss the ever-recurring dreadful thoughts of what her former companions brought down upon innocent Americans five years ago.

"I'm traveling cross country. I can shake my team and be in Carbondale by six tonight. But I don't want a fuss or others to know. Can we meet alone?"

"Oh, Michael … what a surprise. Tonight, alone? Yes, yes, I can do it." Fila could feel her heart racing. "Can you tell me …"

"No, no. I can't tell you anything now," Michael quickly replied. "You just pick a private place, anywhere out there you can get to at six. Keep your phone on. I can track you by your phone's GPS. I have to go now. Remember, six p.m."

Fila put the phone down, suddenly feeling part elated, in part wondering. *I haven't seen him in so long. He's been so kind. My bedrock. What's it about? John Striver? Alone, without others? Where? It's not dark til 9 -- maybe the Sopris trailhead. Perfect. How do I get there?*

For the next several hours she had difficulty paying attention to the voluminous notes she had sprawled out in front of her, various paperweights protecting them from flying away in the slight breeze. She was thinking the trailhead was only a little more than three miles away. Today's hikers would be probably gone by six as they all start out early in the morning. He wants me to keep this quiet. *I can walk there!* Following the main road through Carbondale, Route 133, the road is flat and easy to walk with its wide shoulders. About two miles after leaving town, a left onto Prince Creek Road to continuing onto County Road 6A to the trailhead, marked as a parking lot for the trail to Thomas Lakes. *An easy one hour and a half walk, but I'll leave at four just to be certain. I can't wait to see him!*

"Mary! What on earth are you doing?" Lily's voice interrupting Fila's faraway thoughts. "Your papers are all over our table, and you are just staring off in to space ... or is it your daily infatuation with Sopris over there? But anyway, can you make room for my breakfast. I slept late and I'm starved." Lily, no make up on and in her full-length bathrobe, may have appeared harsh but she was always in a good mood around her beautiful young tenant. There was something mysterious about "Mary" – to Lily, she often looked sorrowful, but well of course, her young friend was shot and is paralyzed, but she was also at times lively and pleasantly conversant. There were no unpleasantries in their relationship, and thank goodness no chatter about missing out on romantic encounters, or worse, finding a husband.

"Sorry, a mess I know. I'll clean up and join you for a cup of coffee," Fila countered with a big smile.

"Hey, now that's a very special happy face. What's going on, dear Mary?"

"Oh, it's just a beautiful Saturday morning, and I'm looking forward to going to the grocery store with you."

"Right," replied Lily with a smile, "and hey later on you know there is a special rock concert at the fairgrounds. I think late this afternoon. You in?"

Fila had to think quickly. "Oh, sounds great, you go. You have so many friends, and I promised Zach I would get over to

Basalt this afternoon. His family is going somewhere and he'll be alone."

Lily's face took on a more serious tone. "You know, you have been amazing with that kid. I know he stuck up for you and got hurt, bad, and you want to return the favor, the sacrifice he is undergoing -- you have been a complete gem. So caring of him. You must be an angel."

"Far, oh so far from it," Fila laughed. "That boy -- he has a heart of gold. He took me in when I was lost. I told you the story what happened after 9/11 – no family, nowhere to go in all the chaos. Cold and hungry, I knocked on his door – just to take a break. We connected, in a mental sense I mean. He was just out of college - - very smart, very empathetic. His father wanted no part of me with their loss of so much in Basalt. He just wanted to take care of his family and the needy there around him in the community, not some stranger like me. But Zach stuck up for me, and then his mother, a good Christian, agreed. All was good … until the shooting. The family became so solemn. I felt so guilty. I had to change my life. Oh, I've told you all this before."

"I know. I'm just so glad we met by Zachary's bedside. Who knows what knucklehead I might have now as a tenant," Lily replied, smiling warmly, reaching her hand out to give Fila's a gentle squeeze. "But, someday, you have to tell me where you were from originally and how in the world you got lost."

Fila tried to act nonchalant after that remark and simply responded, "Sure, we'll do that."

———— • ————

Fila could not wait. At 3 p.m. Lily said bye and was off to the rock concert. Fila washed her face and redid all her make up. She paced the floors – her bedroom, into the small living and the common dining room and kitchen, outside onto the spacious patio, and back again, over and over. She went back to the bathroom, readjusted her makeup, brushed her long black hair again. In her mind, she repeatedly brought thoughts up of what happened nearly five years ago. *I slammed this guy on the head in the stairwell; could have killed him. I almost shot and killed his wife. He claimed I saved the day by shooting that mad scientist who created the deadly Ebola virus and was about to shoot us. He took me in, vouched for my pardon even though the military wanted to try me as a foreign terrorist. I came to America to kill. I shot a young Marine in the knees. Yet this Michael talks to me, tries to build my spirit, tells me I have good in me, wants me to come back. I don't know. I'm so confused.* Now almost quarter to 4 p.m., she felt compelled to head out early, the walk to the Sopris trailhead.

The sun was bright, not a cloud in the sky. The view of Sopris was magnificent. Fila felt strong, elated. It was not a difficult walk, some 5 miles plus some turns on the road up to the trailhead parking lot. Three cars were still there upon her arrival a little after 5:30 p.m. She slowly walked over to a table and bench near the tree line at the start of the path and sat down, feeling her heart pounding in excitement. Over the next half hour, three couples showed up coming down the path to Thomas Lakes. All were chattering, but quickly got into their cars and pickup trucks, and drove off without ever a glance towards Fila. She looked at her phone to be sure it was on and fully charged. She heard a low noise on the road below and glanced at her watch. It was exactly 6 p.m. She felt even more excited when suddenly a large black SUV appeared and drove straight towards her. She stood up as the vehicle came to a fast stop. The driver's side door opened, and Michael stepped out briskly. There he was – looking good, looking energetic. The famous Michael Reynolds, an American hero.

It seemed like an eternity to both of them as they stood still and stared at each other. It had been three years since Michael had found her in Basalt and gave her the satellite phone. They were both thinking that the other looked the same, no aging, but Michael's thoughts then raced to the sensations that this woman was *incredibly beautiful, fascinating, captivating, bewitching.* He had to put these thoughts running through his mind aside before he could approach her. For her part, thoughts again raced through her mind – she knew this man was famous, an American idol, yet *so kind, compassionate.* The emotion peaked when they slowly approached each other and embraced, arms around each other, holding one another closely until Michael detected a sniffle and pulled his head back to see tears rolling down Fila's cheeks.

"Hey, why the tears?"

Fila pulled back slightly and stared right into his inquiring eyes. "Michael, I know we talk so much together on that phone. Thank God you gave it to me, and I'm so grateful for your strength. I have felt so guilty, and I just can't understand how you can be so nice to me. What …"

"No, no, stop. Listen," holding both her hands in his, "you have to first know how attractive a woman you are. Your skin, your hair, your eyes … enchanting, and maybe that beauty has gotten you into trouble with certain men at times, but you have so much more than your outer beauty -- your intelligence, your dedication, your repentance, your, your … and **me**, strong? I have just done what I felt I had to do under times of stress. Maybe I'm just lucky it's worked these last ten years. What I see in you is a deeper character. You are the strong one, your horrific time as a youth, escaping from the Taliban, your seeking peace amid chaos. Okay, so you got brainwashed into thinking America was the prime symbol of evil in the world, but you redeemed yourself, you saved us. We forgive you. I want you to come back and stand tall…"

"Michael, oh I know, but I am just not ready. Thank you, but I have to tell you more about my project. I'm not finished, I …"

"Okay, okay, let's sit down. I have to tell you something first."

Sitting side by side on a nearby bench, Michael began. "First, you have to tell me how you picked this spot to meet. Okay, I did say meet alone, and I'm sure downtown Carbondale would not be the place. This mountain though, it's amazing. It is truly beautiful, reaching up in this valley, all by itself. It's alluring, magical."

"You just answered your own question, Michael. We're alone and it is magical." Fila smiled with obvious joy.

"Right, so the good news, Fila. The state police in Utah identified John Striver from the pictures I had the FBI distribute. He was at a bar where the troopers stopped for a drink as they were just getting off duty. John looked especially suspicious as he tried to duck out but his nervous movements made him an easy target. They took him in without a struggle. We've had the Pitkin County police provide all the information about the shooting. They have Zachary's statement and description of his appearance, and your statement, even his father's damaging testimony. You two don't have to do anything. He will probably get twenty-five years without probation for at least attempted murder in the second degree. I think we were fortunate given the police have been so busy since 9/11, and our courts are barely functional yet." Michael paused and turned his head towards hers.

Fila first dropped her head, then turned towards Michael,

shedding tears again. Her emotions poured out, "Michael, oh Michael, how can I thank you?" She extended both her arms around him. They hugged again, words not needed, and the two sat there side by side with her arm tucked into his, mostly silent for nearly the next two hours in the evening beauty surrounding them. At dusk they rose, and with seeming reluctance Michael drove her back to the edge of town where they said their heavyhearted goodbyes.

Seventeen

ila had to think hard now. *How shall I do this? All this research I've done I have to organize and condense.* She realized it wouldn't do any good to bring her new trusted friend, Lily, into all this, or she would have to confide to her who she really was. The best answer was back to dear Zach, who knew who she was, understood her moral dilemma in trying to sort out good and evil, and who had already helped her in understanding the major religions.

The morning following her Saturday evening meeting with Michael found her spirits quite high. Her heart felt lighter now knowing the crazed John Striver was captured and also knowing that dear friend Michael sincerely cared so much for her well-being, yes, so very much. After saying bye to Lily after their morning breakfast together, Fila followed her normal Sunday routine of catching the bus from Carbondale to Basalt. Lily had asked her how all went with Zachary the day before and Fila simply replied: "Fine, he seems to be improving all the time."

To her pleasant surprise after arriving at St. Vincent's, she was happy to see Zachary there too and for the first time since the shooting. She discovered that Colleen and Grace had pushed him in his wheelchair all the way there, over a mile. After Mass, all seem delighted as they and many parishioners gathered around Zach. Fila was in near tears as she kissed him on the cheek, and she felt grateful and humble that Colleen and Grace had the grace to greet her warmly and give her such strong bear hugs.

"Zach, I would love it if we can soon meet somewhere and I can explain where I am on my ... my search," Fila said quietly to him. "It will take some time, a lot of it."

"Mom!" Zachary replied out loud. "Wait, before we go, I just have something to say to uh ... "Mary." Zachary leaned in close to Fila. "Next Friday, Dad is leaving on a weekend hunting trip. Believe it or not, I can wheel this chair myself. I can get to the library Saturday morning and spend the day with you…. Hey, the weather's warm, the humidity's low – piece of cake, and you don't work on Saturdays, right?" His face lit up.

"Wow, 'you're the man' as you guys say. We're on, nine o'clock Saturday morning."

———— • ————

The weather was warm the following Saturday, and both Zachary and Fila were at the Basalt Library front door for its 9 o'clock opening. Fila had been thinking on the ride over about walking from the bus stop down a ways onto Two Rivers Road and helping Zachary push himself in his wheelchair up the inclining road, but then she thought his sheer determination would be the best tonic for his partial recovery program.

"See, I did it!" He exclaimed to her while looking a little warm and slightly fatigued after his arrival.

"I surely knew you could, dear boy. Now let's go in and get some water and find our usual great spot by the window."

Minutes later, seated comfortably straight across from him, she started: "Okay, Zach," opening a large file of papers and placing them on a small table between them. "Where do I start?

Okay, here. The three big drivers in mankind's history and development have been a combination of religion, politics and economics. And of course the outcome of many, many wars. And certainly, culture and technology come into play too, but my true purpose, my real thrust, as I think you know, is to understand man's, I'll use the word 'man' for all of us, man's behavior. How and why can he be compassionate, cooperative, altruistic and yet the very same person can also be aggressive and violent? Am I not that person as so many others? We'll get to that at the end…. But you know it all begins long before the so-called 'great civilizations' started some seven thousand years ago. We upright mammals, we with the big brains, have been around much longer, maybe a few hundred thousand years. Our long history has a bearing, and again I'll get to that later."

"I'm with you so far, go on," Zach interjected.

"Okay, let's start with the major religions. We discussed most of them before understanding how they started and by whom, but we begged off answering the question **why** man was so disorderly. Now as we said before, isn't it interesting that the six major religions all were formed within about three thousand years, or say from roughly 2500 B.C. to 600 A.D.? Before that, a lot of different kinds of pagan gods were worshiped to try to explain the happenings of man's natural surroundings -- the sun, the seas and so on. Maybe as we discussed before, the sudden thrust of religion was because man had finally developed more sophisticated languages, writing, villages, time to think, to converse, and all that became the background for a few select individuals to argue that this 'modern man' was flawed, was disorderly, and was in dire need of rules, of guidance, or of hope, salvation, forgiveness."

"Okay, so also at that early time," Zachary responded,

"there were tribal leaders, emperors, kings – were they also not disorderly, corrupt, benign or violent?"

"Sure, so wars between them were common when not in that benign stage. Okay, but let me go back. Our genetics. For those many, many thousands of years earlier, we humans were simply another mammal. We protected our basic needs – our mates, our families, our group, our dwellings, and our food supplies with compassion, love and affection. We were benevolent, and group cooperation did more good than one acting alone. **But,**" she emphasized, " we also had our moments of required violence. We had to protect those assets when threatened. So, if another human in need attempted to steal those assets, a rock, spear or club came into play. So imbedded in our human genetic code are both the capabilities to be altruistic, cooperative, but also to be violent, destructive, to physically handle conflict when called for. That's how we behaved – whichever was to our particular advantage at the time. I'll get more into this later, but this knowledge is certainly helping me understand who I really am, the reasons for my own behavior.

"So yes, conflict – man lives with inescapable conflict. Maybe 99% of us want 'love and peace' as the answer to any ongoing, ugly, evil conflict, and that wish, that prayer, that hope is still preached today, but you know, Zach, it's still there – that's what the history books are full of - conflict, wars, fighting, violence, and we still have it today. Some called it the 'evil' side of man's behavior. And unfortunately, as well as violent aggression as being real even today, hey, maybe it's only among the 1%, but it's awesome in destructive power, and sadly it's even a major source of the modern world's so called 'entertainment' for the masses. More about that later, but let's go on.

"Remember we discussed this before, but let's refresh ourselves. The Jewish religion came out of the deserts of

Arabia. Abraham was inspired to seek a land of promise. As we discussed, the Jewish religion developed, and a line of Jewish kings followed. The Old Testament of the Bible tells the story, and it is one of being righteous or facing an angry God. Let's face it, Zach, behave or else. Okay, rules."

"I buy that. Go on," Zach replied.

"Sure, the Jewish prophets warned that man can be disorderly and disobedient despite their God wanting them to be peaceful, all the way back to their tale of creation and Adam disobeying, the original sin. Man had to follow God's teaching, his covenants as expressed in the Jewish Torah. Disobedience results in punishment, but nevertheless the Jewish God is loving and can offer atonement as well. Zach, this is not a huge religion, some seven million in Israel, their promised land, maybe six million here in America and about fifteen million worldwide, but one of huge significance, as the Jews have held together in their faith through centuries of hardship. We have to admire them, but again the point is the nature of man to be disorderly and requiring rules. Okay?"

"Yeah, we agreed on that before, but man needs some help, Fila, and religion explains why we are here, how we are created, why there is so much suffering in the world, and what can be done about it. I guess it describes a better life outside of our own hostile world, but while we are here let's get orderly, try to live a good life."

"Okay, that leads us to the next Jewish story, after Abraham a couple thousand years and after Moses led the exiled Jews out of Egypt and was taught by God that his people should obey God's Ten Commandments. Actually God gave the Israelites 613 laws but the first 10 to obey lay the foundation for leading a moral and good life. Well, Zach, I memorized them because they also are important in the next religion too -- Christianity.

One – worship no other gods before me; two – don't take the name of the Lord in vain; three—keep the holy day; four – honor your father and mother; five – do not kill, meaning murder; six – don't commit adultery; seven – do not steal; eight – don't lie; nine – don't covet your neighbor's wife; and ten – don't covet your neighbor's goods, no theft." Good start, huh?"

"And you are right ... fundamental to Christian faiths as well," Zachary replied with a smile. He seemed to be enjoying Fila's sense of knowledge and purpose.

She continued on. "So this Jewish kid, born a couple of thousand years ago, was named Jesus. It was thought by some at the time that his mother Mary was a virgin, a miracle and sign from God, and that finally the true messiah, the true savior for all, had arrived. Later on it was thought by some that he was the son of God, which he never expounded but never denied. His key message was a little different than Judaism. It was that by believing in him and his father in heaven that your sins could be forgiven and upon your death your spirit would go to join Jesus and God in heaven. Remember Zach at the time, most people were poor and the Jews were under control of their high priests and the conquering Romans, so Jesus offered a message of hope to the impoverished. It was a message of forgiveness for your disorderliness not punishment, a message of God's love for humanity. After Jesus was hung to die on a cross for failing to deny that he was the true messiah or the son of God, it is believed by Christians that he rose from the dead and went to heaven and that happening is his offer to believers – the wonderful promise of everlasting life. His word spread by his disciples, and can you believe a couple hundred years later a Roman emperor declared Christianity the official religion of the sprawling Roman Empire.... Okay Zach!"

"So, Fila, like the book we read in college *The Greatest*

Story Ever Told, you have nailed it – sin and redemption. And with mankind everywhere in endless conflict, the need for interventions into man's behavior occurred further east into Asia at about the same time, right?"

"But don't forget nearby Islam six hundred years after Jesus … complete obedience to Allah, God, in nearby Arabia. We covered the strength of Muhammad in developing this religion there with all its powerful rules governing personal, group, civic and national life, stretching from western Africa all the way across the Middle East out to Indonesia, along with its inconsistencies in interpreting Jihad, and it split factions. Again, a religion developed to direct disorderly man, but even today we don't yet have an explanation for why even the devout leaders can practice violence, the art of war."

"We need answers," Zachary interjected.

"And we need solutions," Fila added quickly. "So we have ongoing conflicts in the Middle East -- Arabia, Syria. We have Iran in turmoil. We have confusion with Muslims in China. We have Muslim/Christian violence in parts of Africa. My violent Afghanistan. My people's horrible attack on America. The duel between Hindu India and Muslim Pakistan and neighboring countries. Venezuela. My God, Zach, is there an end to this madness?" Fila's raised pitch in her voice and the stern look on her face alarmed Zachary.

"Wait, wait," Zachary pleaded. "Stay calm. You have done a ton of research, but … yes, madness, but look, I've read that taking 9/11 out of the equation, there have been scholars pointing out that compared to the last century violent deaths are way down, maybe 400,000 a year violent deaths excluding accidental deaths. Now think of 70 million killed in World War II and maybe 100 million killed that whole century."

"Not the point now, Zach. Sure no world wars going on

right now, but think of what we few just did to America. Weapons of mass destruction can now be perpetrated by little groups upon mass populations. It doesn't have to be powerful nations against nations like the last century. What's more, it's the fear of shootings or other horrible violent attacks, either by an individual or groups. Even if it's a small fraction of the world's 7 billion people, we live in fear, the psychology of fear is everywhere and it's horrible."

Zachary looked perplexed. He had grown up in a culture of very little violence in Basalt, but then along came 9/11 and along came this guy punching him and then shooting him. "You're right," he said softly.

"Okay, okay, let's move on to Asia. I'll try to calm my agitation," Fila said.

———•———

"Okay, we reviewed the Chinese; they developed adherents attached to, well they are philosophies as much as religions, Taoism, Confucianism, Buddhism, so now let's look at the largely populated India, mostly Hindu. After the fall of the British Empire, the nation of Pakistan was created in 1947 to host the Muslim population of India. But remember Islam was not a religion until 600 years after Christ while Hinduism was founded some 4000 years ago. Its core beliefs are that truth is eternal, that each person should strive to achieve dharma, meaning right behavior, and that each individual has an eternal soul, meaning the energy or spiritual or immaterial part of us."

"Nice, Fila, that's understandable," Zachary said. "Go on."

"A very nice religion Zach, and not only the world's oldest living religion but the largest, about a billion people. It teaches that human nature is not just about our mind and body, but that we also have a spiritual spark of God within us; that this divine spirit can bring us peace, joy, and wisdom.... Ah, but now we come back to the rules for behavior. We require training to achieve this state, we need the discipline of the right actions, the right temperament, the proper striving, unselfishness, sympathy, prayer, so practices come into play, such as 'yoga'."

"I see," Zachary interjected as Fila paused. "Yes, all these post-pagan religions founded over a short period of time all have the same basic theme – to control or direct man's behavior towards a higher good, often lead by a spiritual entity of some kind."

"Yes, Zach, just think. If each and every human devoutly followed all these individual rules of behavior without the harsh competitions sometimes between them or the divisive understanding of the jihad within my religion, there would be zero violence in the world. Heaven on earth," Fila theorized quietly, looking forlornly down.

"Yeah Fila, brilliant, but the problem I guess you are saying is that not everyone accepts the teaching and practices of these religions. That something inside, something in our human nature, overrides these rules of behavior, or as you say the practices of the various religions or sects within sometimes create violent rivalries, the Crusades and so on."
"For those reasons Zach, I'm not finished. I researched the great civilizations before these major religions were born, for clues to behavior. I've researched the great philosophers for the meaning of life. And I've researched today's great psychologists and neurologists for reasons why we behave as we do. But wow, it's getting late, so you can manage to get yourself here, can we meet again next Saturday without letting your father know?"

"Absolutely, I wouldn't miss it for the world. I'll be here at nine."

Fila stood up, leaned over, and gave Zachary a tight squeeze around his shoulders and a warm kiss on his cheek. For the first time, she felt the beginning of an inner peace. It had been a long time coming. Certainly the warmth of the Gelayes family helped, at least until the shooting of Zachary. The cordial relationships with here apartment mate, Lily, and her boss at the medical facility, Chris, both helped, but now the confidence and support shown in her from Michael, and the bonding with this young intent listener, Zachary, who unbelievably was holding no grudge against her for his paralyzed condition – all this created a new feeling of belonging, of some contentment with life itself. She now felt she was on a serious mission, a purpose. She could feel good about herself. She now understood that while she had been through experiencing deep personal conflicts, witnessing dreadful violence firsthand with the Taliban contrasted with the strong emotional bonds of loving Asa, and then being part of violence all over again with the harmful attacks on Americans, she perhaps could now finally find answers to her dilemma and perhaps even go beyond – to find solutions.

Eighteen

" It's Friday night, Mary. Whatta you say we venture out for a drink and some dinner right down Main Street? Say Mi Casita for some Mexican beer and food. Ok?"

"Well, ok but remember Lily, no loose men on Friday night making passes at you."

"Com'on, Mary. You are the beauty here, not me, and it's been so hard to get you out. Forget the men. Let's just enjoy ourselves. You have been so busy, three days a week working at the clinic sometimes thirteen, fourteen hours at a time, off to Basalt church on Sundays, and God knows all those hours at the libraries, here, Basalt, Aspen. You have yet to tell me what you are up to. One would think you have some strange past or somebody is paying you for a research project or you're an avid reader and never bring the books home, or you had a man like me and don't want another, or...."

No, no Lily dear. None of that. I ..."

"I know. You had a bad experience as a kid, got to the U.S., and then I'm guessing you got lost from your family or your man in the 9/11 chaos and just somehow wandered into Basalt. But I never hear you speak Spanish or talk about your family, or your ex if you had one. You are the mystery woman. I don't mean to pry, but anyhow, I've come to consider you my dear friend. I ..."

"I'm sorry, Lily," Fila cut in. "I know I have become your friend, but I never do open up to you about my past, like you have opened up to me about yours. Yes, it was chaotic, so much so I don't like to talk about it. I read a lot at the libraries to try to get a new hold on my life. Let me just tell you for now that I am getting myself together, and I promise very soon I will tell you everything.... So okay, let's do it. Let's go out and have some beers and dinner."

The two women exchanged warm smiles as they stood up together to venture out.

———————————•●•———————————

Fila was standing just inside the library door as Zachary proudly managed his wheelchair to the entrance at exactly 9 am the next morning. Both knew Fila did not want to be seen outside with Zachary for fear of George finding out.

"I don't know how you manage to wheel yourself uphill a mile, Zach. You are amazing. Thank you so much for coming, and thank you so much for being my dear friend after what I have caused you."

"Stop that. You know I don't blame you. You have enriched my life so very much. Everyone talks about your beauty, but I know that beauty is also deep inside you. I feel so lucky. You know, if I were a few years older, I would have proposed to you a long time ago." He could not wait to see her reaction to what he just blurted out without thinking. But the two simply exchanged awkward glances towards each other as they proceeded to their favorite table by the huge window facing the edge of Basalt Mountain.

"You say that maybe in jest, but you know Zach, I would

have given that some serious consideration," Fila finally said with a broad smile, breaking the awkward moment.

"All right then, so good, where were we last Saturday? You told me you studied some of the ancient civilizations for some clues. Let's hear it, teach."

"Well my boy. It's not very good news. They all had many deities, lots who controlled their natural surroundings, especially their supreme sun god, but also gods to worship for successful wars. They thought they had to please their gods, and the manners of how they worshiped these gods controlled their lives in every aspect."

"Neat, go on," Zachary sat up intently.

"Okay, I'll start with the ancient, no wait, as we said before, man with the big brain, homo sapiens, had been around for maybe a couple hundred thousand years, but it was not until man learned about ten thousand years ago BC to cultivate crops like wheat and corn and rice and domesticate animals like cows, pigs, and sheep that he had the time to sit down in new communities and learn advanced languages, writing skills, to study, think, and invent new technologies. Sadly, including new weapons."

"Interesting. Where did it begin?"

"Well, let's start with the Egyptians. An amazing civilization. Now, I tell you all this, Zach, because these ancients flow into my whole theme of good and evil, advancements and war.

"Because the Egyptians learned to control the fertile lower Nile River to their advantage and along with a favorable moderate climate, the practices of irrigation and flood control came into play so they learned agricultural techniques, and they also began to build close communities, say around 3000 years before Christ. They consolidated these communities under a supreme leader, the Pharaoh, around 1600 BC when they reach their zenith of power. They learned to make flour from their fields of grain, and then bake breads and distill beer. They learned to produce fibers from their plants, make thread and then weave elaborate clothing. They raised cattle, pigs and goats so had plenty of milk and meat."

"Yikes!" Zachary lit up. "All good stuff."

"Right," she replied. "Incredible advancements. And importantly, they learned to learn. They used the abundant stones around them to learn how to build buildings, temples, statues, and the obelisk religious towers that were later stolen and some seen today in downtown Rome. Of course you have seen pictures, Zach, of their pyramids. They believed in the afterlife and the deceased elites had to have great resting places to prepare for that life. Their religion was an elaborate scheme, many deities needing pleasing and especially their worship of their sun god, Ra. Of course without the warmth of the sun they wouldn't have all those luxuries coming from their agricultural surplus. Their legal system developed under the responsibility of the Pharaoh who was responsible for maintaining order, who then used priests to ask the deities for decisions on right or wrong. So the gods were involved in keeping man orderly on earth, but in addition there was a prevailing belief that there was immortality after death -- in a spiritual form outside the body. Can't get away from that theme, huh, Zach?"

"Yeah, right," Zachary replied as Fila continued.

"But! All that wealth and the advancements in their writing, language, arts, and architecture produced rivalries beyond the control of the unifying pharaohs. Civil wars and territorial disputes within the civilization boundaries were common, and then that very wealth attracted many outsiders. The Syrians, the Libyans, and the Persians all invaded and reduced the empire, the final straw being the Greek, Alexander the Great, taking over in 332BC. The great city at the mouth of the Nile becoming the capital, now called Alexandria, the place of continued learning and center of Mediterranean trade."

"Wow, how did you learn all this?"

"Wait. I'm not done yet. But the Greeks were. The Roman Empire was relentlessly expanding. Its conquest of Egypt was complete by 30BC but ongoing conflicts continued, even Christians moving in or locals being converted by 50AD. And you remember your Bible studies Zach. Jews were there for 200 years before their famous exodus around 1300BC. What a history, huh?

"So let's move over a bit. You know where Iran is. Long ago, it was the Persian Empire, another great early civilization. It hit its pinnacle of power around 550BC. The Empire controlled a vast amount of territory at that time – parts of Afghanistan, Armenia, Syria, Turkey, Iraq, Egypt, Libya, Palestine, and even parts of Greece. Much of these lands were acquired by conquests. Then the inevitable decline – wars with the Greeks, conquests by the Arab Muslims hundreds of years after Christ, the rise of the Turkish Ottoman Empire, and they even lost ground to Russia years later. The Persians were ruled by a number of dynasties without having one outstanding religious overtone. There were the typical attempts to understand the nature of the universe and the nature of man, including of course my theme – understanding the good and the bad in man's behavior. But again, the conquest of lands for power, essential needs and wealth for the few all required the use of violent force."

"Right, so what's new?" Zachary added sarcastically. "Big Persia, now little Iran, still sees violence in its spread of terrorism in the Middle East. And can you believe that now, in our modern times, it has a huge religious overtone. Since 1979, that nation has been ruled by a theology, a religious leader as the Supreme ruler, and a strong set of rules and punishments for man's daily behavior."

"Okay, so maybe your American freedom is better, but we'll talk later about all the violence you have here. I've been watching a lot of your TV movies now that you're back on line and reading older newspapers. But lets move on, Zach, further to the East. A brief word about China. Excavators have found evidence of homo erectus remains over a million years old and of homo sapiens, that's us with the big brains, some 100,000 years before Christ. But writings of humans go back to just a couple thousand years before Christ to the Xia Dynasty, then a long series of dynasties following, but the point is for hundreds of years this vast land experienced long periods of peace and long periods of war. No such thing as everlasting peace among men.

"A great example is one Genghis Khan, 1200 years before Christ. The first of the Great Khans, rulers of a huge empire starting just above China, in Mongolia. By bringing nomadic tribes together under one military rule in Mongolia, they created a force to expand their empire, the largest contiguous empire ever in history, acquiring land and goods and luxuries by the massacre of civilians, creating enormous fear, terror and destruction. These were very tough guys, Zach. Their reach included China and then all the way west to the Adriatic Sea in Europe. They savagely took advantage of any weak state that was in a period of decline as their whole pattern was based upon a nation that was organized for war against others. Talk about God – this line of Khans believed they had a divine mission, to rule all, to tolerate no resistance, to punish resisters, to seek violent revenge against those who had fought back."

"Gruesome. I guess that didn't last too long, thank God. I don't see how that could have been a divine mission, but you made your point, Fila. Understood, and we've already discussed Asia's major religions, all attempting to find the good patterns of behavior required for the peaceful, enlightened man. The opposite of the Great Khans, huh?"

"So we keep going East, Zach. Some scholars have suggested certain Asians crossed an intercontinental land connection some 40,000 years ago and settled throughout your Americas. So maybe there are no truly native, no indigenous Americans. We all came from somewhere, maybe Africa. Anyway, your many so called Indian tribes, the name Indian coming from Christopher Columbus thinking he had discovered a new route to India when we learned the earth was not flat, all had chiefs and warriors. So I guess like most civilizations, periods of calm and periods of violence were common. But further down some outstanding early civilizations did take hold, and lasted until the Spanish explorers came looking for gold and spread their viruses not yet prevalent in these Americas."

"Yes, but wasn't there fighting as well between the explorers and the locals?"

"Well, of course, Zach. That too. Isn't that the nature of competing man?" Fila now giggled as Zachary sat back and smiled.

"Okay, okay, go on, but I'm glad you're not making this a morbid journey describing man's history."

"So, we have the Mayans, the Incus, and the Aztecs. All were outstanding civilizations in terms of art, architecture, fine writing, mathematics, calendars and even astronomy. For a couple thousand years before Christ the Mayans were advanced in farming techniques but also developed a number of cities, often in conflict with each other leading to violence despite their large number of honored deities and divine kings. These deities pervaded their daily routines and often had to be placated, even leading to the sacrifices of human life. It was common practice to use the blood of prisoners of war to feed their deities."

"Ugh!" Zachary exclaimed. "Gross."

"Well, it all began to unravel as the Spanish showed up about 1500 years after Christ. But while the Mayan Empire dominated southern Mexico and Central America, slightly further north was the Aztec Empire. I read it was in power roughly from 1300 BC to again the Spanish arrival 1500 AD. Same thing – advanced agriculture, outstanding art, and architecture and sophisticated in the trade of goods. But like the Mayans – wars among the cities for control of lands and trade and wealth."

"Wait!" Zachary interrupted. "All these advancements all over the world. Periods of peace, maybe goodwill among men. Periods of great deeds and progress in technology, farming, communications, art, literature, architecture. Man is advancing from the cave, from the hunter-gatherer. Man is developing religions to guide the learned towards a more perfect good life. Could it be, Fila, that while the masses were generally poor and had to scratch to survive, that all his violence, this fighting, and these wars were all due to a few powerful individuals who rose up and perhaps were genetically strong in body or willpower or personality -- they became leaders of groups -- they were called kings, pharaohs, chiefs, rulers, whatever, who then sought to increase their standing, their personal possessions, their valuable resource at the time called land, or their competitive power over others -- whatever, these few guys may be the blame for it all?"

Fila sat back, an astonished look on her face. After a long pause between the two as Zachary sat motionless, a look of exasperation on his face, she answered. "Okay, I agree that's part of it. But many of these strong leaders also were instrumental in leading all the advances you mentioned. Many were benevolent, looking out for the welfare of their group. The closer the group, the greater was the cooperation among them. Let's just say for now, those strong leaders had it both ways, and don't think for a minute that without leaders, each group however poor would not find room in their short lives for violence."

"So good leaders, bad leaders, and everyone else too. Is that what you are saying?" Zach responded.

"Yes, and I believe many leaders had both attributes, depending upon the circumstances. And I'm saying the common man then had the same instincts as their leaders, just not the resources to conduct wars themselves."

"I'm getting a little lost, Fila. Can we take a break?"

<hr />

The seasons were now moving into early July, 2026, finding the summer weather in the Roaring Fork Valley delightful – warm, clear and low humidity. Nearly five years after the 9/11/2021 disaster, America was getting close to getting its full electrical power back. Hundreds of thousands of emergency generators were manufactured during this period of need, and most were still in occasional use. The most significant problem was still the full and adequate distribution of food and water supplies. Imports from South America had been essential in the first few years, but distribution channels across the continent still faced a challenge. Michael's early work in leading the trucking industry to have the power to operate was most significant, but some bottlenecks still remained. The amazing fact was how few people died from starving, dehydration, or malnutrition. While new causes of diseases declined rapidly after 9/11, another remaining significant problem still of major concern was the lingering health effects of those seriously infected with the Ebola virus in September 2011. Those who survived infection but were older or had previous health problems had a difficult time regaining their strength. The overwhelmed, overworked medical profession of 9/11 still faced a serious problem in finding enough health providers. The nation's best asset was the old dictum: in times of crisis, man helps his fellow man. Fila had become aware of that noble trait in her frequent telephone chats with Michael.

Despite food supplies coming into the Valley ever increasing, George Gelayes remained busy helping Basalt residents obtain sufficient quantities of meat and fish, while Colleen and Grace were completely devoted to helping the older or sicker townsfolk of Basalt with their daily needs, whether parishioners of St. Vincent's or not. Meantime, Grace had grown into such a beautiful young woman that George was very watchful over her from getting overly involved with the many young men seeking her favors. He seemed to understand anew the lust men feel for an attractive one of the opposite sex, as he had felt towards that terrorist Fila. He could not understand that Grace may have the same inquisitive feelings towards males. Despite her no longer being a growing teenager, George demanded his daughter account for every waking hour. Grace now wished she still had the experienced Fila in the next bed to talk with about the boys and life.

While everyone in Basalt had empathy for the crippled Zachary, there was little anyone including his family could do for him. All thought that his all-out physical effort to roll his wheel chair up the incline to the Basalt Library was outstandingly praiseworthy. George and Colleen thought their college educated son just wanted to continue his learning by absorbing himself in the books of the library. They never though to quiz him on what he was learning or who he was with there. His Saturday trips were now augmented by occasional efforts during the week. Fila had made sure she was getting at least two weekdays off as she was willing to work long hours the other three days at the Carbondale family medical clinic. Lily remained puzzled why Fila spent so much time in Basalt, but could see that probing too much into Mary's busy affairs was a losing effort.

"Okay, my brilliant lady, you have given me great lessons in the earliest religions I knew not enough about, and you have reviewed all those great early civilizations. So you have the answers yet to the puzzle of good and evil you are seeking?"

"Zach, your July 4th celebration in Carbondale and in this town were really nice. Like I told you, I appreciate your American freedom more every day, but no, I don't have a full understanding yet, all the answers, let alone the solutions. Frustrating, but I feel better. I'm getting closer but ..."

"So ... you're not done yet. Go on, what else?" Zach replied softly, urging Fila on.

"Well, I turned to some of the great philosophers and a few great scientists, thinking maybe they have some answers, but frankly not much there. I'm currently reading the work of a great living American professor of neurology. I think he may have some clues, but it's going to take me another week of study."

"Meantime, go on. I would like to learn some philosophy, even though it's from what the Army generals describe you as ... 'an Islamic terrorist'." Zachary looked for a laugh from Fila thinking he was lighting up the conversation, but Fila frowned and looked down.

"Zach, I don't think that's ..."

Zachary would not let her finish.

"I am so, so sorry. I realize that was not funny. The last thing in the world I would do is to hurt you. I …"

"Zach, not another word. I love you dearly. I know you didn't mean any harm. This is not easy for either of us. My background, my situation, my cause of your harm. I just want to be a good person. I want reasons and I want answers, meaning solutions. I know all this is serious. I wish I had a sense of humor, but all I know is my past, and then the love I have received from your mother, your sister, from Father Jensen, from Lily, from Doctor Chris, even from Michael Reynolds, you know who keeps wanting me to accept the presidential pardon I have and come back, but especially dear Zach, from you. I want more than anything that you will walk again. I …"

"I will, Fila, I will. You have helped me so much in finding an inner strength. The doctors keep telling me there is a chance I will heal, that I will walk again. I have that faith that my God is with me. He will help me heal."

Fila stood up, leaned around the back of Zachary's wheel chair and squeezed both her arms around his shoulders, giving him a long, warm kiss on his cheek. "Okay, back to work", she whispered. Zachary reached out and squeezed her hand tightly. Returning to her chair, Fila started. "We talked about Confucius in terms of Chinese religion, 500 years before Christ, although he can also be regarded as an early philosopher, thinking how to bring order out of chaos. He concluded man needed to cultivate an inner enlightenment, to nurture righteousness and virtue, to begin with himself, then spread it to his family, and then to the governors of the state, and then finally peace to the world. Ah, Zachary Gelayes, I wish it could be so.

"So shortly afterwards, we know the early Greeks were quite the smart guys too. Despite their various city-states having recurring civil strife including the Athens/Sparta wars, from

1200BC to 600AD. They produced some real brilliance. And some of that brilliance carried over to the dominant Romans shortly after Christ.

"The string of smart guys, I have the notes here with the years, starting hundreds of years before Christ, first with the philosopher Socrates, 470 to 399, then the father of medicine Hippocrates, 460 to 370, then Plato, 429 to 347, then Aristotle, 384 to 322. Let's start with Socrates. He was poor. He suffered hardship. He wrote nothing. His living simply told his story. He was devoted to the civic democracy among the learned in Athens at the time while he distained the chaos of ongoing wars. He studied the order of the natural world and believed the secret to peace was to seek knowledge of that order. The intellect could then produce a practical use of wisdom, which in turn would produce goodness, for one to be pious, moral. He believed every man had a soul, an internal force that lived forever and that the soul had to be nurtured and was the difference between a good happy man and a bad man. Wisdom nurtured the good soul.

"Socrates went further, into the world of politics. He voiced expressions that politicians had the responsibility to promote fellow citizens to be as good as possible, that leadership needed men who were tutored in this knowledge of morality, justice, and equality. He founded the expression 'know thyself' and believed **reason** would be the force to apply knowledge to all. He carried his honesty to his grave when after being convicted of arguably corrupting the youth of Athens, he passed on the opportunity to escape, stuck with his principles, and was executed."

"Geez," said Zachary. "What a reward for his noble thoughts."

"It gets better," Fila countered. Let's go to the brilliant Plato, also in Athens. He learned from Socrates to seek the knowledge to understand the difference between good and evil. To avoid what he deemed as confusion in the definition of morality, he wanted to establish absolutes, to develop a systematic approach to a way of life that would be rational and ethical. His thinking, Zach, becomes a fundamental to the development of the so-called Western culture.... At first he wanted to be a politician, but he gave that up to establish an academy whose students would pursue philosophical and scientific research. He expressed the need to control one's passions, that parents and state officials had to teach and express good behavior, and for all to strive towards a rational, moral personality. He remains famous today for his stance that good, moral societies can be achieved by the top leaders becoming all-learned and wise. Philosopher-kings he called them."

"Ha!" interrupted Zachary. "If only that could happen. Good bye violence."

"Right. Plato disdained violence. He wrote that virtue was the answer, that it could be attained by knowledge, which could be taught by professional teachers. Moral excellence, justice, wisdom, courage, temperament. But he understood not every man could achieve this state of wisdom, even though knowledge was teachable and virtue taught, but that man often had conflicting motivations, and not all could achieve this rational, moral behavior. But! If the great statesman could achieve wisdom, then society could be peaceful. A nice philosophy, Zach, as you said, but never lastingly achieved unfortunately on this planet. Even Plato towards his end when he was aged began to believe it was written laws that were required to control man's behavior, and that perhaps goodness and wisdom had to come from the divine. Bit of a switch."

"Wow!" exclaimed Zachary. "What a guy. You know, from all we have talked about so far, early civilizations, the big religions, there seems to be a common thread running through all this. Man by his nature is very disorderly. He needs rules of behavior. He needs to seek and find wisdom in order to achieve righteousness. He believes in the separation of his physical body with a spirit inside, his soul, and that this soul can have immortality."

"On the right course, Zach, but let's go on to more philosophers and some scientists and see what they have to say. The last of the famous Greeks shortly after Plato was Aristotle, later known as the source of wisdom in Western civilization. He was upper class Athens, the son of a doctor, schooled at Plato's academy. He believed in logical thought, in creating rules for how to think in logical terms. In politics, he believed that kings and leaders, in order to do good, should learn from wise philosophers. Professional philosophers would understand what is necessary to sustain life, then advance to the arts to refine life, and thirdly advance the art of politics to attain the good life. Essential in this process required learning practical science and making laws that were bound to ethics. He wrote that the smart politician would use logical means to examine all the facts and circumstances in various different complex situations and then arrive at the best course of action. And of course he believed in the immortality of the soul.... Oh, and one more thing – violence. We can't escape it, can we, Zach? Believing in Greek superiority, especially over the rival Persians, he tutored 13 year old Alexander, who later became Alexander the Great leading his armies from Egypt all the way to Afghanistan."

"Neat! Let's take a break. You have all that in your notes?"

"I'm just summarizing from my notes, and I have a lot more in my head," said Fila. Let's get some water. I have some snacks.

Look, I have a long list of philosophers and scientists, but I'll just review a few with you, okay?"

"Listen, my head's not full yet. You keep going, and you know I want to be here with you til almost dinner time at home," Zachary replied.

<hr>

"All right, let's get started again. We're just trying to understand the nature of man, the ways of his behavior and then the reasons for it. I'm moving past the so called Dark Ages, not much went on there except of course my guy Muhammad starting Islam 600 years after Christ, and its sometimes forceful spread east to Indonesia and west to Spain.

"Well, at least there was one key philosopher, Avicenna, known as the most influential of all the Muslim scholars. Born 980AD, as a precocious child, he had memorized the Koran by age ten, later studied logic and medicine and wrote a long book 'The Book of Healing' referring to Plato and Aristotle and containing logic, psychology, geometry, astronomy, math and music, but no ethics or politics. He continued to write extensively. His 'Canon of Medicine' became the most famous book in the history of medicine. Of course God comes into play. He thought of God as the essence of everything, our existence, but that with the development of self-knowledge, an individual becomes a freer person. Not much on violence here, Zach.

Let's get back to morals and behavior. Move ahead to 1517 when a German Catholic priest, Martin Luther, rejected several of the practices of the Roman Catholic Church, and upon failing to renounce his writings was excommunicated by the Holy Roman Emperor and condemned as an outlaw. He taught that good deeds do not promise eternal life but is attained as a free gift by God's grace and faith in Jesus. He taught that it is God who forgives not the Pope, and that the Catholic church should not sell forgiveness or pardons for money. He translated the Bible into German and married a woman. His writings spread throughout Europe and were the basis for the Reformation and the start of Protestantism. He rejected philosophy as unsatisfying since it did not teach about loving God. He did not believe in Hell. He did believe the Jewish Ten Commandants were important on teaching Christians how to live, although he did not accept Jews because they did not view Jesus as divine. Now this is really something, Zach. Here's a strange answer," she smiled. "He thought Islam and violence were the work of the devil."

"Incredible, his diverse thoughts. Okay, so all your work is done. Put aside your studies. All this violence, yesterday and today. Simply, the work of the devil. That easy to understand," Zachary smiled.

"So where is this devil and how do we get to him? Isn't that the hard part?" she laughed. "So maybe all these smart guys I'm studying may not have the answers I'm looking for…. Let's go to another famous theologian in his prime around 1250AD, Thomas Aquinas, also a philosopher as he embraced the thoughts of Aristotle, and attempted to pull together his teachings with the principles of Christianity, reconciling reasoning with theology. He spent much of his time between Naples, Italy and Paris, France with some time in Rome as a theologian. He wrote that while man could achieve knowledge without divine intervention, he believed that man needed divine help to reach the ultimate truth. Example is that he thought while man, while utilizing reason, could achieve the virtues of prudence, temperance, justice, and fortitude, he needed God's help to achieve the virtues of faith, hope, and charity. So ultimate Truth is found through the combination of reason and faith.

"Pertinent to us, he did reflect on war and violence. He believed the law should be used to promote good and to avoid evil. Monarchy was all right but should be curbed since popes had a moral authority over kings; that Christians should be pacifists unless defending themselves; that wars were just only as a last resort and wars for expansion, pillage, to convert infidels, or for glory were unjust. He went on, describing the nature of God as perfect, infinite, the cause of all things, the creator of the orderliness of nature, the mover of all things in motion and his free gift was offering eternal life. He explained the nature of sin as being contrary, evil. That Christ rising from the dead was to offer another way to restore humanity to a path of salvation who was otherwise sentenced to die because of his sin. So his lesson was towards teaching that man's happiness, his goal in life, towards doing the right, moral things and achieving everlasting life, but even if a sinner, that a reward is gaining redemption through Christ. Pretty good message for 800 years ago., right Zach?"

"Oh that disorderly mankind. Yeah, good there were thinkers like that who had such an influence on the Christian church. He became a saint."

"Now let's jump to the early 1600's. A Frenchman, Rene Descartes, sometimes known as the Modern Father of Philosophy, uttered the famous statement 'I think, therefore I am'."

"Neat," uttered Zachary. I like this guy."

"He was well educated, strong in his Catholic faith, wrote poetry, and studied mathematics. He later began to travel extensively as he felt he wasn't sure he was certain about anything. He thought he could observe man and nature, and then meditate and maybe he would find 'truth'. He developed a vision of linking all human knowledge into one universal wisdom. Maybe with long self-training of one's mind, he could develop the power of knowing. This mental discipline could become as orderly and rational as mathematics. When I think Zach how this applies to behavior, it seems he was saying that although we have the free will to be good or bad, if one has a true knowledge of the what's about him, this rational wisdom, he will act with moral behavior. A well-applied and trained mind can attain truth and certainty. Again Zach, a similar theme, East and West, old and new.

"Around the same time frame in England as its pure monarchy was transforming into a constitutional monarchy with as strong parliament, an English philosopher named John Locke became known as the advocate for 'freedom' before the courts of law, in religion, in expression, and in the press. This is important - contrary to prior thinking about man being born disorderly, Locke believed the human nature of man is that each individual is a moral being, that government should protect that, and that such a trait is protected if man achieved self-reasoning, knowledge, wisdom. He wrote that government and politics are necessary, but so is the liberty of its citizens. That while human nature controls behavioral actions, the practice of learning knowledge is the highest ideal. And while he never wrote a book on his great interest in morals, I think, Zach, this is pretty uplifting since he was rebelling against societies' widespread upheavals of the 17th century…. I guess this would imply wise men don't fight and unwise men fight."

"Nice theory, but we'll need some evidence of that," Zachary answered. "Perhaps many very high I.Q. people are not really wise, meaning they are missing the wisdom all these guys have been looking for."

"We'll see," Fila replied. "One plus one equals two. The empty brain plus wisdom equals moral behavior? A lot of dumb people conduct themselves on moral grounds. How bout the Jewish moral commandment for everyone, smart or dumb - 'thou shalt not kill'. Lots of smart people with vast knowledge in their heads can be very immoral."

"Remains complicated, huh?" Zachary shrugged.

"I'm going to get there, just may take a little more time. Now, right after these guys, a brilliant natural philosopher comes along, Isaac Newton, a mathematician, physicist, astronomer, theologian. He accumulated great knowledge and thought things out developing laws of motion, gravitation, mechanics, and a mathematics later known as calculus. He was a true genius. Philosophically, he conceived of the universe upon natural and understandable laws, but interestingly, Zach, religion also comes into play here in his thinking. He is quoted saying 'Gravity explains the motion of the planets, but it cannot explain who set the planets in motion. God governs all things and knows all that is or can be done'. I really think that is a profound statement from such a genius, and…"

"Right on," Zach interrupted. That's my religion, that's my faith. Yes, God governs all things, but He has given us free will. We can be good or bad, moral or immoral at our choice. The religions are just there trying to guide or direct us to make the right choice." He looked up eyes wide open begging for a response.

"Zach, I don't have answers yet, but I'm glad you are strong in your faith. Stay firm. It's so complicated. Let me go on…. Remember out of the dark ages we were all taught in school the period of how the European Renaissance dawned. Incredible art, and the genius of Leonardo daVinci. Popes and kings and religious leaders of every religion were dominant at the time. But later the turmoil of the 1700's brought a new age, the Age of Enlightenment. The new thinking undermined the influence of monarchies and helped create amazing new architecture, especially places of worship. But not a lot of free thought about religions. In Europe and America, the concept of 'reason' was to be the main source of advanced ideals, such as freedom, progress, tolerance, constitutional government, the separation of church and state. Great thinkers became famous as newspapers became prevalent. Men such as Bacon, Descartes, Hume, Kant, Rousseau, Adam Smith, Voltaire, Benjamin Franklin, Thomas Jefferson, James Madison. The thought of the rights of the individual and equality among all men became new liberal thinking. The thoughts of natural rights, such as individual freedom being universal, but Zach, few of these men were atheists. Example, Voltaire said that without a God who punishes evil, the moral order of society was weakened.

"Now I still have a problem with all this advancement. Even without laws or customs, the scholars said all men have equality and freedom as natural rights. But these learned gentlemen could still not explain the reason for what they called evil, immorality. Gaining true knowledge was supposed to be the way out, but man and societies continued their violent ways no matter how much learning progress, from this 18th century thought to this very present day.... The renowned proponent of free market capitalism, an economic system which could increase the wealth of all workers, his reputation as 'Father of Economics and Capitalism', Adam Smith. He was also a moral philosopher. At an early age, he developed a passion for reason, free speech, and liberty. In 1759 he published his 'The Theory of Moral Sentiments'. He believed morality would develop as humans embraced empathy, mutual sympathy for the other guy's feelings and personal situation.... Again, great thoughts but not the final solution for me."

Fila let out a long deep breath as Zachary stared at her in awe. She continued. "So I liked studying David Hume. A little different. He wrote 'A Treatise on Human Nature'. He was a skeptic to practical reason, but rather he expounded that passions, meaning our emotions, govern human behavior. That our minds only perceive what we receive impressions of, coming from our experiences and also what we feel.... So this guy was an atheist. It was simple – our passions produce or prevent moral actions. Reason not a factor."

"Now that's a twist," said Zachary. "Emotions, passions. So the guy shot me without any reasoning. His morality or lack of it had nothing to do with it. It was simply his overriding passion for you, and I was interfering."

"Getting closer. Next time we meet, we talk about this angle. I'll give you a hint. The son of a wealthy doctor in the mid 1800's became interested in natural studies, religion and philosophy. He took a long voyage and witnessed nature's huge diversity. He concluded that every species attempted to replicate beyond their means, and that only the fittest survived as mutations had them adapt to their environment. The theory of evolution. Important Zach. This guy, Charles Darwin, later wrote 'with all these exalted powers Man still bears in his bodily frame the indelible stamp of his lowly origin'. That's profound as we will see the next time we meet."

"I can't wait. Tomorrow?"

"I'm working at the medical center all day tomorrow. The day after, 9 am?"

"I'll be here, for sure."

"Okay, before we leave, I'll just give you one more thought, just to let you know how hard this subject is even for the most brilliant. You've heard of Albert Einstein, the genius who described particles and energy, the motion of molecules, and forecast the development of the atomic bomb but advised President Roosevelt against using it as a nuclear weapon. He was agnostic, no firm belief in an afterlife. As a pacifist, he favored a democratic global government, a world federation to put a check on the power of nations, something as we know Zach the United Nations is unable to accomplish. He left an expression I quote: 'Without ethical culture there is no salvation for humanity', and a year before he died, a Jew by birth, he said: 'For me the Jewish religion like all other religions is an incarnation of the most childish superstition....'"

Fila paused and looked intently into Zach's eyes, whose face grew into a frown.

"Okay, like we said. This is complicated."

"Right, and as one living philosopher recently stated that you and I have to think about, Zach ... quote - 'is there a common standard of moral justice as deduced through reason based on what rationality serves human necessity?'"

"Now how did you memorize that?" Zachary queried as the two broke their discussion for the day.

Nineteen

It happened the day after Fila had worked 13 hours at the Carbondale Family Medical Practice helping the continuous stream of patients coming in and going out physically and administratively. She was back at the Basalt Library continuing her conversations with dear friend Zachary about the history of mankind and why man has been so violent from the earliest of recorded history, the great ancient civilizations, to this day, 2026.

George Gelayes had been feeling ill, tired and weak, for several days. He was anxious to get back to his daily routine of hunting and fishing, helping less able Basalt residents meet their protein needs. Even with the vast improvement in economic conditions over the last several years, regular full-time jobs were still scarce in the valley, and economic sharing was still a mainstay to survival. An interesting human trait that in times of great need, the spirit of helping one another, of sharing, and of helpful cooperation were all outstanding human qualities, and the closer in relationships or vicinity, the stronger that trait.

George had heard good stories about Dr. Chris Stanford's medical prowess and decided to set an appointment with him to determine if a reputable physician might be able to speed his recovery. It just happened that Chris was seeing Lily about the continuing pain in her knee that day, her appointment time just after George's. Dr. Stanford's examination of George included an electrocardiogram to test for heart problems and an examination of his full body for any signs of possible tumors. He conducted a blood test to look for other anomalies, but those results would take a few days to read. He concluded George probably had a lingering virus and gave him several samples of an anti-inflammatory drug along with some pain relief pills.

As George was leaving Dr. Stanford's inner office, he bumped into the waiting Lily who was standing amidst a fully occupied waiting room holding at least a dozen patients. She was speaking quite loudly to a nurse standing in the middle of the room. "Did I tell you, my roommate Mary works here, off today but you must know her. She is such a beautiful woman and works such long hours here at the clinic three days a week."

"Right, right," said the nurse smiling. "She's a terrific help." And then Lily added that Mary's good friend in Basalt, a young man, had been shot by a stranger on Two Rivers Road and was now crippled, and Dr. Stanford was helping him in his recovery. Clearly overhearing this conversation, and just as Chris stepped out of his examination room, George's blood suddenly began to boil as his face turned red.

"Mary! Mary! That's no 'Mary'", he exclaimed. "That's the escaped terrorist from Afghanistan, named Fila. The one who came here to kill on 9/11! They claim she is pardoned, but don't trust her. I know she is supposedly living here in Carbondale, but what she did to my son is unforgivable. I can't, I can't…" The tone of his voice subsided, but he clearly was a man in pain.

The three key listeners, Chris, Lily and the nurse all stood speechless, but all sitting in the room looked up aghast, just staring at George in the middle. George took a deep breath and calmed his emotions. His head lowered. He said nothing more as he proceeded to walk briskly out of the medical office, his facial expression of one clearly perturbed.

That evening Lily felt helpless to confront Fila as they had always communicated so warmly with one another. All she knew was that Mary had spent the day with that man's crippled son at the Basalt Library. She had to think this out as Mary, or is it Fila, had always been a mystery to her and to Dr. Stanford.

"Well, dear Zach, old boy. I can wind this up this morning and next time tell you some of my conclusions."

"Conclusions, conclusions! I thought they were illusory," he replied. "Nobody gets to the bottom of violence. The only conclusion is to have a simple faith, like me. Believe in the everlasting life of one's spirit, one's soul, through a belief in the goodness of your God, and here on earth just pray that reason will ultimately prevail."

"Nice were it that simple, but the question remains. Why do we still have violence on this earth no matter the good intentions of the overwhelming majority of the human race. The law, the police, the religions, the customs, the morals – but we still have it. I'm getting the answers Zach."

"Yeah, and then what? You said you need solutions, Fila." Zach said firmly as Fila stared back at him, speechless.

Fila tried to lighten the conversation. "Okay young man, let me dazzle you. I reviewed the tapes and read the writings of one renowned professor of neurology from Stanford University, one of the world's leading neuroscientists named Robert Sapolsky. He wrote this maybe twenty years ago, but it's still profound today. But I'll dazzle you some more before we get to him," Fila smiled as Zachary finally warmed to the conversation.

"Today's world has been shaped so much through the

incredible influence of one man's thinking back in the mid 1800's. His name was Karl Marx, the one who wrote the Communist Manifesto. You know class warfare and violent clashes between the 'have's and the have not's have been going on for a very long time. Even your Jesus when the masses were 99% poor railed at times against the privileged high priests. Kings, emperors, czars, governors, chiefs were always the privileged, but always the small minority.

The German Karl Marx was a man of everything -- a philosopher, historian, sociologist, political theorist, journalist, social revolutionary. But because of his extremist political publications he lived in exile in London. Observing the huge differences in wealth and labor among men, he concluded that human societies develop through class struggles, and that there is ongoing conflict between the large number in the working classes and the smaller number in the elite ruling classes. He thought this tension would eventually lead to a societal crumble, and that socialism would then prevail, where the state rather than the capitalists controlled the means of production. He went on to predict that this society would be eventually transformed into a classless society where communism would prevail, you know Zach, 'from each according to his ability to each according to his needs', but he went even further. Impatient, he urged that actual revolution against capitalism was needed to speed this process.

"Why do I bring this up? It's because he was so influential in the course of history. His message led to massive violence in this world. The Russian people's overthrow of the czars soon opened the door to the small followers of Marx to take control of Russia. The take over was extremely violent. Then China became Communist, Cuba, Vietnam. Adding the insane Hitler to the mix, in the 20th century some 100 million people died as a result of all this violent competition. And this Jew named Karl Marx turned Lutheran turned atheist was a mental genius. He studied everything. Forget philosophy and ideas, he thought – the world was run by materialism. Get physical to make it happen. Revolution!"

"Geez, Fila. You're getting emotional here. Stay calm."

"Sorry. I'm just mad. And still mad at myself for allowing my getting taken in by crazy propaganda. Here I was the one searching for peace, and yet I became a violent revolutionary. Karl Marx – ha!"

"Just shows you the power of the soapbox," Zachary replied as he reached out to touch her shoulder.

"Okay, I'm good, I'm good now. Let's move on to Sapolsky. I like this. He ties our biology into our behavior. He says it's the working brain that triggers our behavior. But he believes it is very complex as to why in each individual the brain can trigger different behaviors. There are relationships to one's environment, one's senses, one's hormones, brain chemicals, nutrition, early childhood experiences, and stresses. Each of us has a nervous system extending throughout our brains and then down throughout our bodies that are unique and different in performance than everyone else.

"Let's start at the cellular level. Our some 200 billion brain cells, or neurons, each of us having a slightly different number, may be resting or in action. Each cell stands alone with some 10,000 receptor sites receiving chemical messages. The messages proceed down a long body of the cell electrically, but only if stimulated enough, to some 10,000 terminals out. We each have a slightly different number of receptors and terminals, and they can change over time. When in action this process takes energy, like only 5% of our body weight is our brain but it consumes 25% of our calories, and requires lots of chemicals like sodium and potassium. So this amazing line of neural messaging can operate differently in power, in intensity, in action, one individual to the next. To make this system work in a space where all these neurons are not actually touching each other is the role of our chemical transmitters, our neurotransmitters. These guys, like glutamate which put calcium into our neurons to speed their work, can be different individual to individual as to how they are made, their reacting to too much sugar, or to energy depletion, or to short term stress or chronic stresses, and they can change over time in any one person. So the whole brain doesn't work in a straight line function, but by complex pathways, angles, feedbacks sometimes back up the chain instead of down, variances in the transmitters."

"Whoa! This is all new to me," Zach exclaimed.

"Well, to me too," Fila replied.

"So our brain is in parts, each with different functions. We have an automatic part moving our organs and limbs, but that control comes from a sensing part, and then we have a bigger frontal cortex part which is larger than other mammals which provides reasoning feedback and control over our emotional part coming from or starting with our senses, you know of sight, sound, smell touch and hearing. So our big brain allowing thoughts and memory and reasoning, as opposed to other mammals without a big frontal cortex, means we humans can change our bodily functions just by thinking! And this process has tremendous individual variability. This thinking and our resulting behavior generally means our bodies are acting in a way in order to maximize our own self-interest or advantage, but not always. We have these other chemicals also in control, in our bloodstream called hormones, or in the spaces between our neurons called neurotransmitters. This vast array of hormones is made in both our brain and in our bodies. Their role is to transmit messages. And they even work in the brain since our neurons also have some hormone receptors. The chemicals acting as neurotransmitters also greatly affect how we behave as too much of this one or not enough of that one can regulate how we behave at a certain time. Zach, you've heard of the feel good transmitter 'dopamine' depending upon what we eat?"

Zach stared blankly.

"Okay, so all this variability impacted by differences in hormonal and neurotransmitter chemistry, emotional settings, different environments, early experiences even in the womb, changes over time, number of cells active, diet and health of the individual. All impact differences in behavior, but let's get to the big one to find out where aggression and violence come from – evolution and our genes. As man evolved over hundreds of thousands of years, two important genetic traits stand out for his survival. One was to allow competition and aggression, and the other to allow for cooperation and altruism. We had to competitively protect ourselves from harm – not only protect ourselves but our mates, our families, our group. And a male finding females to preserve his genes with offspring, protecting those offspring, protecting or fighting for his food supply and his dwelling areas, and conversely on the other hand, we had to garner support of those around us to help us succeed. Two hands are better than one. So at appropriate times we could be aggressively violent. Then at times we could be very cooperative and kind. These traits are embedded in our genetic code, our DNA.

"But our DNA sequence, our inheritable messaging system as to who we are, changes over time. Unintended or forced mutations which were beneficial helped us survive. The environment at the time perhaps controlled how our genes responded. We humans have all these external factors coming in through our senses, to a focal point in our brains called the amygdala, the center of our emotional responses, and luckily those messages can be sent up front to our frontal cortex which can provide some reasoning, some restraint on the wrong action. But that focal point of our five senses can also stimulate good or bad actions immediately through stimulating more testosterone, more stress hormones, less serotonin – and different, individual to individual as I explained. So different emotional settings can cause different reactions one person versus another. As Sapolsky says 'we don't hate violence, we just hate the wrong kind'."

"And so I say in response dear Fila, as we progressively evolve to a more peaceful world, our genes will lose the more violent side of the competitive state we inherited. Violent aggression will be screened out," Zach smiled.

"Ah, so we wish. But societies are wired to competition. Beyond the individual, we also have group violence where even one person can stir up a whole group to be cooperative or conversely aggressive, You know, group benefit societies or group riots. Your sports, movies, prizes, businesses, trade, everyday life, even if mostly peaceful can turn aggressive. Hockey fights, you know? Nice if this competition did not have to reach the violent stage. I brought up Karl Marx. He said 'in a world without deprivation, you would have no aggression'. I don't think Adoph Hitler would have paid any attention to that advice. No, I think Sapolsky is on the right track. Evolution has weeded out violent behavior over males competing for females. Most societies today with their early teaching of rules and standards of good behavior certainly help. Societies with rules of law making violence illegal, religions teaching violence is immoral all help. 'Help' I said Zach, but not eliminate. Advances in medical knowledge teach that impulsive aggression can be separated from premeditated aggression and treated differently, that serious neurological defects need compassion and treatment, that normal versus abnormal behavior can be better understood, that each individual is biologically unique. Sapolsky hopes this better understanding will lead to more mutual cooperation and altruism, and that violence is our worst nightmare.... So now it's my turn Zach. I'm going to draw my own conclusions and then look for a place where the solutions will find me.... Maybe."

"Can I tell you how much I love you," Zachary spoke softly holding out both his arms to her. With those words, she hugged him and began to cry, again.

Later that evening with Lily, the dinner conversation together was again friendly, warm. No mention of who this 'Mary' was in reality, just periodic cautious glances at Fila from Lily's curious eyes. But the next day at the clinic was to be quite different. While Dr. Stanford seemed to be in a state of confusion, perhaps disbelief, his nurse who had overheard George's rant was unable to keep this startling revelation from every clinic employee and every patient within reach. And of course a dozen patients had heard the outburst the day before. There was no secret anymore.

Fila had spent the first two hours that morning at her desk completing paper work on that day's patient list. It was not until she walked into the patients' waiting room that the cold stares and murmuring overtook her. Tension filled the air. The nurse who Lily had been speaking with the day before wasted no time in front of six patients and two other clinical staff members to confront Fila in a loud bold voice. "Is it true? Mary, Fila. You are the escaped terrorist from the 9/11 attack? We all heard it on the news, over and over -- an attractive young woman who shot one of our Marines and almost killed the wife of our great Michael Reynolds. Your accent is not from the Caribbean, but from an Asian country. Am I right? You name is not Mary. It's Fila. Right?" But silence. Everyone was trying to listen, then staring and searching for Fila's reply.

Fila's face shuttered. She looked stunned. She was speechless, motionless. She was obviously unaware of George's outburst the day before. At that very moment, Dr. Stanford entered the room and broke the silence. "Mary, come into my office, please right now."

Quickly closing the door to his office behind her entering, Chris Stanford paused, seemingly searching for the right words as he sat down behind his desk. "Sit, sit down please…. I have a hard time believing this. You have been such an outstanding employee for us. For the last hour I have been overwhelmed. Patients and staff seem terrified. They are afraid of you. The 9/11 attack was horrifying, so traumatic for so many. I, I … please tell me the truth."

Somehow Fila was able to regain her composure. She knew this day might come. This was it. She was ready. "Yes, I am Fila," she said calmly. "Sent here to assassinate the outstanding scientist, Rose Haines, the wife of Michael Reynolds. Our six-person group was to be the insurance policy in case the virus didn't do its job. We mostly failed. The other five were killed. I didn't kill that Marine. I aimed and shot him in the knees, and he has recovered. I could not pull the trigger on Rose. I did pull the trigger and killed the mad scientist who developed the deadly virus, preventing him from shooting Michael and Rose, and I guess me too. For that the president of the United States pardoned me, despite your generals wanting to hold me as a foreign terrorist." Her voice was steady. "I have suffered these past five years, trying to find a new peaceful life, but I am haunted every night thinking about what I did…. Doctor, Chris, I am so sorry. I had searched for peace my whole life after escaping from the Taliban in my native Afghanistan, and then I was brainwashed into believing America was responsible for all the violence in the world. I have learned that is not true, but I understand I have to suffer the consequences for what I have done. I'm so sorry." She lowered her head and then lost it, a soft sob following.

"All right. I understand," said Dr. Stanford quietly, sitting down in another chair next to her. We have to let this calm down. Let me give you a month's pay and maybe you can just stay out of sight awhile, and we'll see what happens. I know there are people here who have befriended you."

"I cannot cause you or your practice trouble," Fila replied. "I will go, yes. Thank you so much for giving me the opportunity here. I, I …" and she again fell silent.

Later that day, when Lily entered the living room to the shared apartment, the two stared at each other momentarily. "Lily, I have…"

"You don't have to tell me … Fila! I already know. Here's the problem. Landlord Edwards caught me on the way in. News travels fast. He said the other tenants have already gotten to him. He cannot have a so-called 'terrorist' in his building. He wants you out, immediately. I drove over to Zachary's house and told him what had happened."

"Lily, I…"

"Stop, my friend, I know the whole story. Your buddy – Zachary. What a great kid. He loves you for who you really are. Thank goodness his father was not home. He told me everything from the beginning…. Listen, I have a plan."

"Lily, you don't have to do anything. I have been blessed with your kindness."

"I said 'don't talk'. As people get to know you -- it's been five years, things will simmer down.... Look, I have a friend who has been looking for someone to take care of his house and dogs. His wife died, and he wants to visit his daughter in Los Angeles for a few months. It's a great house, about two miles down 133, you know towards your beloved Mt. Sopris. Very isolated. No one will know you're there. And I trust him fully. I can get you in there tonight. It's not dark til nine." Fila was speechless, but her facial expression at last changed to one of relief and gratitude.

It was an easy ride. Fila had quickly packed her clothing and her few possessions. They reached the secluded home of the elderly Charles Bodine by 8 that evening, still quite light. The house was quite substantial, surprisingly nice in a somewhat isolated area. Down Route 133 from Carbondale about a mile, a turnoff onto 111 Prince Creek Road, which turns into Route 5, a sharp turnoff onto Stark Mesa Road, and another turnoff onto dead-ended Cabin Drive Road. Here Mt. Sopris in the evening turned into all its majesty – only about 4 miles away.

The introductions were easy. 'Charlie' as Lily called him seemed a real gentleman. Lily simply told him that Fila had some serious past problems but now was quite fine and an upstanding young woman, not to worry about a thing. It was obvious that Charlie fully accepted his good friend Lily's word. 'Mary', now 'Fila' to Lily and to Charlie, was given a spare bedroom for the night, and Mr. Bodine was off to the Denver Airport early the next morning. Fila spent an hour on the phone that morning petting and catering to the two Labradors while catching Michael up on the whole story. Lily promised to bring groceries to her every Saturday while also promising to tell Zachary the story of where she ended up, safe and secluded.

* * *

But it was two weeks later on a Sunday morning that Fila received a very pleasant surprise. The dogs barked, and Fila stepped outside to see Lily's car pulling in the driveway. Odd, she thought, as Lily had just come by the day before to drop off some groceries. Someone else was sitting in the front seat. She drew closer, and there was Zachary, a mile-wide smile on his face. The two women quickly removed his wheel chair from the back seat and cleverly helped remove Zachary from the vehicle and onto his chair.

"You two have a great day. I'll be back at four to take him home." Fila did not hesitate to put both her arms around Lily and hug her tightly.

"Why are you so good to me?" Fila asked with glee in her voice, as Lily just simply smiled broadly.

Zachary cut in, "We Christians cannot forgive an evil act, but we do forgive your spirit within you Fila. That's who we are."

A half hour later, the two were sitting comfortably outside in the warm summer sun, not too hot and low humidity. Kind of perfect, thought Fila.

"Zach, I could tell you about the thinking of some more noted philosophers and scientists, but I think we have enough. I can now draw some conclusions."

"That's fine. I'll just mention one I came across myself that's recent, and I think fits your theme, Fila. A historian, 67 years old, named McClay, recently said 'Conflict is part of the human condition and can never be eliminated. Neither can the desire for power and the tendency to abuse it.'"

"Right on Zach. I like that. But can we have the ongoing

conflict without the violence sometimes attached to it? I've done my research. I know I'm being repetitive, but…. Conflict from day one to today. Mammals over food, mates, and territory and for us humans constant conflict it seems over everything … except for those many welcome moments of cooperation and empathy when everybody benefits. So the sociologists state that this century is so much better than last when 100 million were killed in major conflicts, but you know my little group could have almost matched that number. In today's technologically advanced state, we proved that a small group can develop or possess weapons of vast mass destruction -- nuclear, chemical, or biological. WMD's you call them. The planet is infinitely more potentially dangerous, but even without that threat so many people live in fear. There are some 400,000 violent deaths per year, a very, very small percentage of the world's population, but nevertheless fearsome and tragic and on people's minds. In the United States where mass shootings are measured by four or more persons injured or killed, there have been over 250 incidents recorded the last 50 years. These shooters are of all ages and backgrounds. They can take place anywhere. The only common denominators found so far is that many may have suffered a childhood trauma, have grievances or a recent personal crisis, have access to firearms, have studied other shooters, and may have had a serious, at least in their minds, unsettling conflict with others. Some 18,000 people a year here are shot dead, well below the annual death rate from drugs or driving, but still gruesome to witness.

"So okay, Zach, let's face it, about man's behavior. Let me summarize. The scholars of the past believed man to be inherently disorderly. He needed rules of behavior so that society could progress out of the chaos. The poor guy is flawed. The ancient civilizations forced a lot of deities upon peoples' daily living habits in order to keep order within their societies, yet wars among nearby groups prevailed. Jealousy over power, competition for food supplies, pushing for greater territory, material goods, trade route advantages – many reasons for this technologically advancing man to fight…. Then in a short period of time after that phase, the major religions came into play to try to tame this disorderly man. These religions all had and still have their personal and group membership virtues, but some also clashed with one and another and still do today. And we cannot forget that ideological differences among smart men also played a role in violent times, and such competition still keeps the world armed to the teeth today -- despite the goodwill charter of the United Nation calling for peace in the world of nations. And finally, today we also have to keep in mind the threat of weapons of mass destruction falling into the hands of small groups, just like the small but rich and resourceful group that attacked America and sent me here. Sorry, let me ramble on."

"Yeah, you're on a roll," Zach said with a slight smile.

"The problem is that not everybody follows their culture's rules, their religion's tenants, or the common guidances of centuries of great philosophers who preached that gaining knowledge, wisdom, and enlightenment would lead to a higher state, one of goodwill among men and peace. Again, noble in thought, but many cannot ever achieve that higher state, or to the contrary many who do become smart still have that trait of using violent power to gain what they want. Then the neuroscientists come along and teach that all behavior starts in the brain, determined by a mixed influence among many factors -- genes, womb and childhood experiences, environmental impacts, nutrition, differences in number of brain cells and cell receptors, varying chemical compositions or quantities of hormones and brain transmitters, susceptibility to change including accidental or forced mutations … and, that each one of us can behave differently in responding to the external forces perceived by our senses, or as I told you before even prompting behaviors with just by the way we think. It's very complex!"

Zachary simply stared at Fila, in awe, then found the words. "I don't mind you telling this story over and over. It's profound. So if every person on the planet -- religious, agnostic, atheist, philosopher, wise, uneducated -- each and everyone of us – simply lived within the rules, the laws, the ethics, or the moral teachings of their particular societies, we would then have peace on earth?"

"Well, you said **every** person. Wishful thinking, my dear friend. So, sure, but in reality, not sure if even the leaders of all societies believe in all those rules, and also remember, Zach, while man can be inherently cooperative and altruistic, he can inherently show those sudden flashes of aggressiveness, no matter the rules."

"Okay, you now so bright Fila – you're saying the great majority of us are law-abiding, moral, peaceful, but the exceptions are the disruptors. Could it even be 99% to 1% in today's advanced societies? You yourself were a peaceful, moral, rule abiding young woman, then became the violent exception. How did it happen and what are you going to do about it?"

A long pause in the conversation followed, Fila with her head down, Zachary staring, waiting for a response. "I don't know yet, but enough study. I'm going to pray, to whom I don't know, but I'm going to find some solutions."

The studies were complete, their long conversations over. It had been all summarized over and over. The two sat in silence, simply holding hands in the warm early afternoon sunshine.

Lonely days followed. It was moving into August. It had been difficult reaching Michael on the satellite phone. He was always so busy. Fila was fascinated with the beauty surrounding her, and what comforted her the most was gazing at the ever-changing light on nearby twin peaked Mt. Sopris. She started taking walks to the trail base of the mountain, the spot where she had met Michael. An hour over, an hour back. She observed hikers returning in the late afternoon, overheard conversations that it was an all-day hike up to the summit and back, and a fairly difficult climb the last few hundred yards. She dreamed that she should make that hike, all the way to the top. But Lily's latest visit changed all that.

Twenty

The word had spread to Basalt. This lovely young attractive woman named Mary who had been so kind in the community, helping Colleen care for the needy at St. Vincent's, was actually the escaped female terrorist from the disastrous 9/11 attack five years earlier. Didn't the Gelayes family know that? How could they have taken her in? Why wasn't she turned into the authorities? Her good deeds, her kindness, seemed to be quickly forgotten. And the tragic shooting of young Zachary Gelayes was all her fault. And where was she now? Everyone seemed to know that Zachary's father stringently forbade his son to have any further contact with her.

The word next spread throughout the Roaring Fork Valley. In Carbondale, residents praised Dr. Stanford for quickly discharging her, but the questioning of Lily persisted. You removed her from your apartment but where did she go? Is she a danger? Is she gone from the Valley? Lily simply responded that she had no idea of this woman's whereabouts, but that she had shown no intent of harm to either her nor anyone else. In fact Lily reported that she had been a model citizen and was surprised as anyone else upon discovering her true identity. She pleaded but to no avail that perhaps this stranger with the accent was seeking forgiveness from God and was trying to redeem herself.

The days, the weeks, continued lonely for Fila. There was occasional television reception at he Bodine home, and Lily had shown her how to tune in. When she was able to view a news report, it seemed the headlines were usually about a violent incident somewhere in America or the world. It saddened her all the more. Thank goodness for the occasional calls through to Michael, who continued to plead for her return. Still not ready she would reply, but she thanked him over and over again for his generosity in sending to her friend Lily a $5,000 check for her to cash and use for hers and Fila's expenses. By mid-October the weather was turning cold and snow flurries were often in the air. The peaks of Sopris were now white again. Fila stared at the changing panorama for several hours every day. Her walks to the trailhead became less frequent as the weather became colder, and after listening to Lily's lament, she was glad no one there over the summer had recognized her.

On one of Lily's Saturday visits, Lily broke the bad news that if heavy snowfalls on Saturdays continued, she might not be able to drive through to the Bodine home, but the good news was that Mr. Bodine was about to return.

"But does that mean I must leave? Where…"

"No, no," Lily interrupted. "You are safe here. Zachary is telling no one, and I certainly am not. With winter coming, you are fine right here. I was able to reach and confide a little with Mr. Bodine. Told him the story you knew the 9/11 terrorists but you are out of a job and needed some seclusion, but with something to do. You know, Charlie, you can call him that, is a very kind soul. We have been friends for a long time from some charity work we did together years ago. I told you his wife had died. Tragic. In a car accident with a speeding truck. Hard to get over. It's been ten years now, and he is getting older. I think he recently turned eighty. I told him how kind you are, and that any of your 9/11 involvement must have been a personal mistake, and that you have been making amends for it. I told him you have been a dear friend to Zachary and to me and that you are 100% safe to be with. That people around who don't trust you are misunderstanding. We just need some more time for things to settle down. So the good news is he agreed you can stay here until your situation is resolved. He is grateful you have taken good care of his home and dogs…. Okay?"

Speechless but with a hint of tears in her eyes, Fila reached out and gave Lily a long, tight hug. *Why do I come to tears so much,* Fila thought to herself.

———————— • ————————

Charles Bodine somehow was able to get a lift home through the snow- clogged roads. Of course the kind driver delivering him believed the house empty and had no idea there were dogs in the house or that the missing "terrorist" was inside as well.

Fila was overjoyed to greet him. "Welcome home, Mr. Bodine, Charlie," she exclaimed.

As the dogs pounced upon him to add to the royal welcome, Charlie smiled broadly. "Well, well, looks like my home has been kept well and my pups look healthy … thank you, thank you, Mary, or should I call you by your real name – Fila? Lily told me your story."

Fila's smile ended abruptly, and she lowered here eyes to the floor.

Charlie, a very sturdy, alert, handsome senior with wavy gray hair barely diminished, quickly sensed Fila's change in demeanor. " I'm sorry … now, now," he said. "Look, I trust Lily, and we know it's all going to work out for you. She said she doesn't know your full, complete story, but she told me all the time you spent with her, you're … you're fine, gentle, and kind. I asked her to come over tonight. She's hoping her car can get here through the snow. She is going to bring some dinner over and stay the night. No work tomorrow…. If we want, we can all talk together.

Fila nodded and raised a slight smile.

That evening the dinner chat centered upon winter life in the Roaring Fork Valley –- the variety of food supplies continuing on the rise, some ski areas open with few out of state visitors but plenty of locals, schools fully functioning, available electricity getting close to pre 9/11 days, employment on the rise. The talk was positive.

"Come on, you two," Charlie said. "Let's go in the living room and light some candles." Minutes later as the three sat comfortably, he began. " You know my daughter in LA is a nurse, and she really enlightened me. She said compared to our valley here which got off easy, LA was hit pretty hard with that virus. It apparently was a genetically engineered version of the deadly Ebola virus, which previously could only spread by contacting bodily fluids. It was kept alive on some type of chemical dispersant and able to spread to humans just like the airborne cold viruses. These guys somehow spread it through the whole city, but luckily the virus died off quickly, and then…"

Charlie paused as he sensed Fila again pointing her head down, her face lips tightening. Lily sensed the mood. "Hey, we don't have to talk about this, we can just…"

"No, no. Let's talk," as Fila grimaced, "let's get it out…. Yes, I was sent here actually as one of the terrorists. We came here to destroy you Americans. If cutting your power off with that nuclear explosion, the electromagnetic pulse bomb, and spreading that virus didn't act fast enough we six, armed with AK-47's, would assassinate your key leaders and give the virus time to work. But your daughter must have told you – a smart guy named Michael Reynolds quickly learned that certain vitamins could fire up a person's immune system and overcome the virus, and when those vitamin supplies soon ran out, it was learned as your daughter told you that the virus was found to quickly desiccate as it fell from that special chemical dispersant where it was kept viable. Our geniuses failed to think the fatality rate would end up so low a percentage of you Americans." Fila's face looked stern, bold, then turned sad. She began to weep, her head down, tears flowing uncontrollably. *There I go again.* Lily quickly grasped the situation and moved next to her on the couch, putting her arms around her.

"Go on, go on," Lily said softly. "Let it all out."

Charles Bodine sat motionless, his eyes wide open staring at the two women. Fila sensed the warmth of Lily's touch, the same warmth she felt five years earlier when the Gelayes family took her in. She regained her composure. "Five of us were killed. I somehow survived. I could not shoot my assigned target. I now know why, but I did shoot a Marine in the legs. He's okay now. I don't know, but anyway, an American scientist was the one who had designed the virus. He was about to kill us all, and somehow I shot him before he could shoot us. I was told I saved the day. I was held in house arrest at this Michael Reynolds' home and told the new president might pardon me, but I felt guilty. I had to leave. I thought I could get to the Pacific Ocean and leave your country, but I only reached here, and that wonderful boy, Zachary, and his family took me in. They knew who I was but disguised me, gave me the name of Mary, had me help at their church. It wasn't until that mad guy tried to take me away by force and then shot Zachary that things turned around with Zachary's father. I was put out. Then I met Lily… kind Lily, Lily I'm so sorry, I'm…"

Charlie remained transfixed in his chair. "Fila, Fila, don't be sorry," said Lily. "Okay, enough talk about your past now. I wanted Charlie to hear it. It's over. It only upsets you. Come on, tell us what you have been doing at these libraries all this time," said Lily. "All your meetings with Zachary. Please go on."

Fila nodded, pausing a few seconds, getting herself together, but could not avoid having Charlie know her full story. "But so you understand…. I was raised as a young girl in very hostile, violent surroundings in my native Afghanistan. The Taliban ruled with an iron hand over we second-class women and also governed with tight rules over our men. I lost much of my family to senseless violence. I finally found a group hiding on a small island who all wanted nothing but peace. It was my dream. I was so lucky to escape there. I was happy, happy, but then the leaders brainwashed us into thinking that it was America holding up the possibility of peace for the world, that you were evil, that you were responsible for the world's violence and had to be destroyed. They had wealth somehow and could buy advanced weapons, missiles, scientists, and then as I said I was handpicked to be their insurance policy… crazy, crazy, it was all wrong. I know you have some bad here. I see your television news. I know what happed to Zach, but most of you Americans are kind, generous, peaceful…"

"No, Fila, don't cry again," said Lily while Charlie continued staring dumbfounded. "We understand. We are forgiving people to those who repent. I only know you one way. I've come to love you. But again, all that time in the libraries, here, Basalt, Aspen. What is it?"

"Okay, I'll try to explain. This Michael Reynolds…"

"Yes, yes, we all know the name," interrupted Charlie. He was now into the conversation. "The brilliant young engineer who saved the day during the abrupt warming climate crisis and then became the head of the big National University after 9/11 in Denver."

"Yes, that's right, and I consider him a dear friend. He wants me to come back, but I've told him the same story I'm telling you now. I wanted to find out why we did what we did, why I thought I was a person of peace and then turned violent. How can mankind be so compassionate and kind one minute and so aggressive and violent the next? And the same person! Doesn't have to be two different people. So I go to the libraries to read, to study, from the beginning of civilizations to today. We're the same now as we were then."

"And you found your answers?" Charlie queried. It was now Lily who stared dumbfounded.

"Yes, Mr. Bodine, I have, but I want more. I also want to find solutions. I thank you both for your kindness, but yes, you two can turn me in, you can, but I pray I just have enough time to find some ways which will prevent future violence. I was misled before as to who and what was holding up world peace. I want to learn it myself, dear Charlie, dear Lily. I pray you give me the chance."

A long break in the dialogue ensued. Each of the three looking away as the candlelight reflected off their solemn faces. Finally Charlie spoke up somewhat forcefully. "Young lady, you stay here as long as you like, as long as it takes for you to find your answers. I like your honesty.... But you have an uphill battle. With my father in the Second World War and the Korean War and me in the Vietnam War, yeah and they still go on, all I know is these wild ideologies cause a lot of problems. The Nazis thinking they were the superior race and wanting to conquer all of Europe and Russia, then the Communist propaganda that Marxism was for the whole world, even if by force, and the radical Muslims believing their theocracy is the wave. I just don't understand it. Maybe young lady, God will speak to you like He did to Moses and Muhammad."

Charlie smiled with that last comment, and Fila was able to show a slight smile of gratitude in return. Another pause in the conversation, then Lily. "You have my support too. Go for it, but I have a question. So if you find your solutions, if you find them, then what?"

"I understand what you're saying," Fila answered. "All this cannot be just for me, to make **me** feel better. Michael, Michael… You should know. You never see it, but I keep it charged. It's a satellite cell phone Michael gave me. We keep in touch. I want to tell him everything. He is very influential. Maybe just maybe…. And if I do find solutions to reducing violence, I'll tell him, and then I want to face the music. I will reveal myself, but I want to tell you both – I am so thankful for your kindness and do not want to burden you any further. I'll go back when it's time."

Lily put her arms around Fila and the two again hugged a long time as Charlie gazed admiringly at his old friend Lily and his new friend Fila, the beautiful Afghan woman hiding out in his home. There were no more tears. He suddenly felt very important. It felt good.

———————— • ————————

As late winter turned to early spring outside Carbondale, Fila used Charlie's welcoming ear to rehearse what she was going to tell Michael, all that she and Zachary had concluded about the long history of man's violently aggressive behavior interrupting man's other pattern of virtuous altruism and cooperative behavior pointing towards periods of peace for most and advancement in the human condition for some. She knew it was repetitive for her, but Charlie was hearing it for the first time and was appreciative. It was a review of the ancient civilizations that advanced forms of art, architecture, writings, language, agriculture, hunting weapons, clothing, housing, and other necessities. Many worshipped an array of deities largely representing the natural world. Then the short period of the emergence of the great religions designed to teach or construct orderliness to a disorderly man, some through the belief in one supernatural God, some through the belief in philosophies on how to conduct one's life with beliefs in an eternal spirit or soul within the human physical body. And then to periods of what was called the Enlightenment, the worth of the individual, not just the state. But still the concept of evil prevailed within those who disobeyed the rules. There were and still are some who simply don't follow the rules, whether of their state, their religion, or their particular culture's laws or customs of morality. Charlie had never heard that the modern 20th century witnessed 100 million persons killed by wars.

By June, 2027, Fila was calling Michael every day. It was only perhaps once a week he could find the time to listen to her, usually late into the night. "Michael, so I've told you. Most of us are good, moral, helpful to others, cooperative with our friends and neighbors and communities. We've developed all these rules, all these laws, all these codes of morality to enforce this goodness, yet violence persists in this world. You see there has always been conflict. That's the common denominator. We just can't always resolve conflict peacefully. All these motives for aggressive behavior – we are acting, behaving, for our own personal advantage, real or perceived, for our personal gain as a trait of our natural inheritance. It may then relate to attempting to gain power, an advantage over others, that natural trait of competition built within us, or of seeking control over others, of seeking money or material goods, of jealousy, revenge, or suffering illusions, or believing in a radical ideology." Again the words were repetitive to Fila, but she thought Michael might come to a new understanding, a reason why his America was attacked. It almost seemed as though Fila was reading from her notes verbatim as she spoke to him.

"Wait, wait, Fila, I think I've got it, but you are going so fast." Michael rubbed the phone against his ear as he frowned. "Slow down. You've learned so much. Are you at Charlie's? What's he doing? Are you still getting along with Charlie and Lily without that common denominator of conflict you've been talking about?"

"Yes, yes. Charlie's asleep," she laughed. "And for sure there is no conflict in this wonderful home. We are in the peaceful cooperative stage!"

"Okay, so I want to hear more about this neuroscientist approach. They didn't have that in the old days. Man was just sort of good or bad, and then you're saying they needed rules to try to bring order to the bad. You know – good and evil. Moral or immoral."

"Right, Michael. It's on the right track. Since we have been around from homo erectus to homo sapiens with this larger brain, particularly the larger frontal cortex compared to the another mammals, maybe for a couple of hundred thousand years now, we have been evolving from having those basic genetic traits of aggressive competition for our mates, and then to protect our selected mates in order to preserve our species, then to protecting the security of our place of living, and then to protecting our food supply without which we cannot survive. So that's the need for our aggressive behavior side, to then the other side, the altruistic, cooperative genetic trait to improve upon our family's, our group's, our tribe's position though mutual beneficial help. That's you, Michael, to perfection…. But the aggressive side has been more in men's genetics as the stronger sex, and the cooperative side more in women's genetics as the bearer of babies and caretakers of children."

"I guess you mean that more or less historically, right, because men and women have both traits, no?" Michael quizzed.

"Yes, both sexes have both genetic traits despite their key hormonal differences to preserve the species, and of course today you know, I see your TV and read your magazines, the lines between men and women have narrowed significantly here in America."

"Well, yes and in much of the world. Maybe your religion Fila, Islam, is still behind that trend."

"Let's not talk about that now, Michael, please. So let me go on…. When so called 'ancient history' was over and so-called 'civilization' began some eight to ten thousand years ago with the advent of agriculture, domestic animals and preserved writings, there was great progress in technology – farming equipment, architecture and huge structures, beautiful buildings, places of worship, new religions, the start of philosophies, means of transportation especially ships and of course more recently with trains then cars, then airplanes. We were using our big brains, Michael! But the point here is our big brains were also causing lots of trouble – more advanced weapons all the time in the wrong hands. The neuroscientists can now describe in intricate detail how our brains cause, determine our behaviors. I mentioned to you before about these inherited traits, our genetics, but then we have to add the differences in our brain cells, sensory messaging, chemical hormones and neural transmitters all unique individual to individual, responding differently to childhood experiences and environmental influences…"

"Understood, thanks," Michael interrupted. "Listen, gotta go now. It's late. Just got a message. Have to prepare for an early morning meeting. Believe it or not, think I can talk tomorrow night, same time. Take care."

"Okay. I'll call. Bye Michael." After her lecturing Zachary, then Charlie, now Michael, Fila now thought she had the answers to why violence. Now she had to find solutions as to how to reduce it.

In the late afternoon the following day, Fila sat Charlie comfortably down in his favorite living room chair, and without hesitation, she exclaimed: "Now you had a great nap after exercising the dogs and whatever else you were doing out there. Stay awake now and tell me if you understand this. This is what I'm telling Michael tonight. Are you listening?"

Charlie smiled broadly and thought to himself that he was really liking Fila's company. They seemed so comfortable with each other that he felt she could say anything and in any way to him and vice versa.

"Sure, gorgeous," he flirted. I'm wide awake, I'm listening and you can talk, just get me a glass of water first, maybe an ice cube and a shot of vodka in it too would be perfect." Fila grinned and hustled to the kitchen to fulfill the request. Her thoughts were 'yes this guy is our typical man', but old enough that his flirtations were said in a spirit of that warm, friendly way. He was not going to pull any stunts. Fila spent the next hour rehearsing what she was going to relate to Michael that evening, that man was flawed, inherently disorderly. But her main point would be to describe to Michael how she has classified all the different kinds of aggressive behavior that end in violence.

Later that evening, Michael was alert and listening intently. "Right, Fila, I'm understanding what you are saying, but don't you think with seven billion people on this planet and after the horrors of war of the last century, that maybe 99.9% of us want to live in peace? We have all these laws, these religions, these philosophies now, so maybe it's just a handful, like the leadership group from your so-called island of Dire, that remain the problem?"

Michael, that's a big point, but it's not the full story. Yes, a small percentage of whatever you want to call it, 'the bad guys, evil', or whatever, but in today's world of advanced technology just look at the massive damage a very small number of the world's population can do. And a bigger unpleasant point no one likes to think about – don't forget the multiple nations having atomic weapons. They just happen to not be using them right now, but what if?"

Moments of silence ensued before Michael spoke. "Yes, well, so I'm still here. Go on."

"Right, okay. So Michael, no matter what, we all have this ongoing element of fear in the back of our minds at times despite whatever amount of current violence is happening at any minute, and I can sense that uneasiness at certain times among you Americans despite the remarkable recovery you all have made these last six years.... So let me try this on you. There are ten different types of violence we should be concerned about. Listening?"

"Shoot," said Michael. "I have my pen and notebook."

"Yes, here I go. Classes of Violence." Fila then spoke very slowly.

"First – between and among nations.

Second – factional civil wars within nations, racial, religious, or political

Third – terrorist groups within and beyond borders.

Fourth – gang related, big and small, organized or spontaneous.

Fifth – criminal behavior, collusive or individual.

Sixth – government corruption, or directed, to exert or retain control

Seventh– Individual psychosis planned or of a sudden rampage.

Eighth – religious or cult or ideology extremes.

Ninth – extended domestic disputes.

Tenth – extended worker disputes.

Got it, Michael?" Fila said

"Wow, you covered a lot of ground, Fila. I have it all down. Let me try to digest all this."

"Thank you, Michael. You do know this – everyone knows your name. You are famous. You are smart. You are very influential…. I pray something can be done."

Another long pause ensued. The conversation ended. *But how can he do anything if he doesn't have solutions?*

Twenty-one

On Thursday July 1, 2027, she had made up her mind. She would climb Sopris. On the Saturday before, Lily had arrived as usual at the Bodine house, again with plenty of groceries. The two chatted awhile about the improving life in the Roaring Fork Valley, and of course Lily had no choice but to mention the stories about this female 'terrorist' which were still swirling, a year later. Fila needed to continue to stay put. But by Monday, July 5th, she made the decision as to exactly when she would hike to the top of the twin-peaked mountain. It would be Thursday. By daybreak Thursday morning, she woke up excited. She was ready. She decided that rather than the typical hikers' non-stop journey up and back, her taking more than one full day was needed. She would stay overnight. She remembered she was Afghan, the home of so many mountain people. Staying overnight in the chilly air would be no problem. She needed time to think, she kept telling herself. She then noticed Charlie up early too, making coffee in the kitchen.

"Charlie, you know all those walks I take to the Sopris trailhead. Nobody has recognized me even though I try not to face any of those climbers. They must all know my name and reputation but don't know what I look like. I…"

"But I would still be careful with those green eyes. You're different, you know," Charlie interrupted.

"Yes, but Charlie, you know how that mountain has me captivated. I look at its majesty so often, every day I've been here, six years. I have to climb it. I have to go to the top, and I'm going to stay there overnight. I've not heard back from Michael in weeks. I have to think clearly in that cold air up there."

"Think about what? When, when?" Charlie asked.

"Now, this morning. I'm going. I'm going to think about what I've told you – man's behavior."

"Wait, wait, it's more than you think if you're going to stay overnight. You need certain things to take." Little did Charlie know of Fila's ordeal walking five nights without supplies six years prior from Denver to Basalt in the late autumn. He had not heard that part of her story.

"Yes?" Fila responded.

"I guess an Afghan knows how to climb mountains with bare rocks at the top, but I have one of those real light down winter coats that fold up. You need some water, some power bars, and I think a medical kit – never know, you might need it. And I have some maps too." Charlie looked intensely at her, seemingly half in surprise and half in admiration. "Wish I could go too. Funny that it's so close, but never been up there. Legs got too old. They tell me not a bad climb most of the way but pretty expert near the top…. But why overnight again?"

Fila reached out and hugged dear old Charlie warmly. "Thank you, thank you, dear friend. I just have to think, up there. Need some time. I don't know…. Hey, you've helped me. I'll be fine."

With her rugged boots on that she had purchased while

living with the Gelayes, long, tight hiking pants, a short sleeved collared shirt, sweatshirt over her shoulders, and her backpack full with all the items Charlie packed for her, Fila set out following Prince Creek Road a short way to Dinkle Lake Road which lead up to the Thomas Lakes Trailhead. She was there by 8:30 a.m. It was about 50 degrees there and probably heading towards the average 70 in the afternoon at this altitude. She noticed about a dozen parked cars and pickup trucks already there but no persons. While the mountain finds some year round hikers including a few who carry their skiis up with them, the many summer hikers usually start very early despite some 14 hours of daylight. They plan for a 12 mile hike up and back and some four hours up from this Trailhead and then another four hours back. Most begin their journey around 7 a.m. She had read many times about this beautiful scene before her. The twin summits, called East and West, both rise to 12,965 ft. above sea level with a saddle between them about 300 ft. long with a 300 ft. drop. Geologists believed the mountain was formed some 30 million years ago by an igneous intrusion, meaning where hot liquid core rock, magma, rises and cools and solidifies before reaching the surface, as opposed to a volcanic explosion. It is one of the largest vertical rises in the continental United States rising 6700 ft. above the Roaring Fork Valley, 10 miles away from Carbondale at the town's 6200 ft. elevation.

Following the sign for the Mt. Sopris Trail and then back and forth upwards for another hour and a half, she reached the still wooded area around the first of the four Thomas Lakes. Fila continued following the trail up the northeast side of the mountain passing many empty camping sites close to the lakes. Charlie had checked the weather forecast for her on his laptop prior to her departure. It called for July 8 and July 9 high temperatures on the peaks of 60 degrees and a low at night of 35, no rain, sleet, or snow showers but some high winds exceeding 25 mph.

Fila broke through the tree line and stopped to take in the amazing views now in sight. Her excitement mounted as she resumed the winding trail upwards, seemingly in a hurry. At first she ignored her feelings of becoming winded as she had waited so long for this moment. But then the climbing became very steep and she slowed down. Ahead was a long trail of piles of white rocks all about, what the locals and reference books called the talus. Then she could see it clearly – the summit, the East peak. She felt no fatigue as she scrambled to the top, letting out a deep breath of joy. The view out over the valley and surrounding mountains was magnificent. She then turned to the west and remembered that from the West peak, one could see the beautiful line of mountains of the Elk Range, including a number of Colorado's famous 14'ers, meaning peaks reaching 14,000 feet elevation above sea level. She saw the trail leading through the rocky saddle between the two peaks just as the wind picked up.

As she walked the connecting path down 300 feet and back up at a fast pace, she noted the so-called 'wind caves' along the way where one could take shelter against the typical strong winds at the peaks. *Later,* she mused, as she hurried to the West peak. In the warm afternoon sun, and trying to ignore the strong wind, she sat and marveled at the wide expanse of this most beautiful scene all around her. She remembered the wonderful mountain expanses surrounding her native village in Afghanistan, but never had she as a young girl ever been to the top of one. Suddenly her mind became clear, focused. She had sudden thoughts which she felt like were pouring into her mind from somewhere unknown. She felt an impulse that she must begin to write them down. *Too windy here, back to the rock cave.* From 3 o'clock that afternoon til she fell asleep somewhere around 3 a.m. with the flashlight that Charlie had packed in her bag still on, Fila sat and wrote on a large notebook she had brought along. She maintained her energy with the snacks Charlie had packed for her, along with frequent sips from her water bottle. She had put on that very light but warm jacket that thoughtful Charlie had packed for her. The temperature near morning must have plummeted into the low 30's. Charlie just had a hunch she would need all those things as Fila's excitement had revealed to him she would probably stay up there overnight, as she had strongly hinted to him.

During those hours nestled in the wind cave, she said to herself over and over: *I'm getting it, I'm getting it. I don't know how or from where or from whom. I am not on the mountains with Moses speaking with God or Muhammad hearing from the angel Gabriel. It's just coming to me. The ten classes of violence. Settling conflict.*

After reviewing her pages of scribbled notes, she summarized it all on just a few. Her key notebook pages the next morning read like this:

<u>Violence between and among nations</u>. America would join with the two other military superpowers, Russia and China, in an alliance with, but not a formal part of, the United Nations. The three nations would create a new military force known as the 'Superforce', a standing army of 150,000 troops divided equally from the three nations of the United States, China, and Russia. The United Nations would still be responsible for providing ongoing peacekeeping troops in situations and at the time when ceasefires went into existence, but the Superforce would be used at the early stages of armed conflict in order to put an end to it quickly. To become a reality, it would take a tremendous amount of sincere negotiation among these

three superpowers to make clear that while the three countries may have different political systems, the ongoing competition among them is based solely on fair economic terms, and that they have a common interest in fostering and preserving world peace for the noble good of all mankind. Not only would the initial negotiation of this concept require the greatest skill in negotiation, but the subsequent follow up in practice as well. The world is divided into almost two hundred sovereign states. The Superforce acting on its own rather than being invited into the conflict would be violating individual state sovereignty unless it were called upon to act by one of the parties – a difficult but necessary negotiation. And would all three superpowers have to agree in unison when to act, or could one superpower veto the actions of the other two? And what if one of the superpowers itself were to have armed conflict with another nation or even within its own borders in a civil war? Such a bold idea would require the utmost in negotiating skill and goodwill to make it a reality, but the concept is golden.

<u>Factional civil wars within nations</u> -- <u>religious, racial, political.</u> Again, the Superforce would be called upon to quickly stop further armed conflict. Details would have to be worked out as to the level and amount of violence initiated in order to commence this commitment. Again issues of national sovereignty come into play. A new United Nations Mediating Commission [UNMC] would subsequently be called in to help settle differences and provide peacekeeping forces. This area would also include peaceful revolutions against existing governments or classes that become excessively violent.

<u>Terrorist groups within and without a nation's borders.</u> The richer group of 20 nations, the G20, in conjunction with the UN would provide funding to support national military forces with the tools needed to stamp out the violent portion of the

terrorists' operations, with always the threat of the Superforce coming in on top. All 193 UN member states would reaffirm their allegiance to the body's Charter Preamble that states the members' commitment to world peace and the Human Rights' every person's 'right to life'.

Gang related, large and small, organized or spontaneous. Interpol, the international police coordination body, would receive increased funding from the G20 to assist each area experiencing outbreaks of gang violence and be publicly accountable for positive results. Coordination with the UN 193 member states, the UNMC and the Superforce would be supplemental if the violent activities are of a larger scale. UN member states would agree that past a certain threshold of violence that local governments cannot handle, their individual state sovereignty would take a second place. Expect much political debate about this issue, but too important not to reach a consensus.

Government directed violence to exert control, to retain control or are simply grossly corrupt. Again national sovereignty would be overcome if a certain threshold of violence is exceeded by using a counterforce through coordination with the UNMC and the three Superforce nations. Basically, with 193 nations in the formal United Nations membership, the ideals of the institution would be overseen, that is enforced, by the powers of the three world's superpowers. A blunt, advanced step, but necessary. Again, a great deal of diplomacy would be needed as most nation states believe their own national sovereignty is supreme.

Criminal behavior – collusive and individual. Large groups as above with gangs, otherwise a local police matter whereby a nation or city within a nation may appeal to the G20 for additional funding. A new group crime committee within the G20 would be established to provide oversight and report on results. Peaceful protests provided law and order.

Religious extremism, or cult extremism or ideology extremism. Again, past a certain threshold of violence, a UN member state may seek assistance or be forced into asking assistance from both the G20 and the UNMC.

Individual psychosis, planned or sudden rampage. The United States would take the lead in developing innovative medical testing using Artificial Intelligence methodology for discerning the state of one's mind in contemplating violence. While 99% of the mentally ill do not commit a violent crime, the search for that 1% potential becomes the challenge. Eventually such advanced tests could be given to every teenager in schools and to those applying for a driver's license or passport or ID card. Persons failing the test would be offered free medical counseling. The debate over individual liberty would be an issue in democratic states but the benefit to society would eventually win out. Where advanced psychiatric medicine shows a clear relationship within the public, especially among the young, of being strongly influenced by the incessant barrage of violent movies, television shows, streaming videos, and video games, the United Nations Commission on Human Rights would initiate a bold campaign to persuade the video makers to reduce the volume and strength of such violent scenes.

Extended marital disputes. An abused spouse would go to court and seek a requirement for the abusing spouse to take or retake the psychological screening test and if appropriate be offered free medical attention or counseling along with a binding desist order. This process utilizing recent advances in neurological science would be a strong extension of the practice some individual states now provide to abused spouses. It would become better and become universal.

Extended worker disputes. Another psychological disorder usually following the discharge of a worker that would

be handled similar to the class above, requiring a terminated employee to take the new innovative test before leaving the place of employment.

Fila's note pad concluded with: "The common denominator in all this violence is the phenomenon of conflict between two or more parties. We have learned that no two human brains are exactly alike and that they can change over one's lifetime in directing their behaviors. Conflict that is not settled peacefully, by compromise, by negotiation, or by clear thinking can often result in violence. The motives for the violence are many – power or control over others, money, goods, jealousy, revenge, excessive greed, excessive self-interest, excessive anger, behaving for a real or perceived personal advantage, acting on false information, or a brain chemical imbalance causing one to recklessly abandon the rules, the law, the norms of society and then attempt to create their own definition of 'justice'. So many voices around the world see violence and then preach out loud that 'love' is the answer. 'We all just have to love each other'. But the problem is a minority number of the world's population don't or won't practice that ideal at any given moment, and as we have seen at 9/11, weapons of mass destruction, weapons of all kinds, are easier and easier to obtain and use. There have to be solutions beyond the noble goal of 'love'."

The bright light of the sun rising in the East awakened Fila. She felt fresh, liberated, her mind free of torment. She had found the answers to mankind's many centuries of violence and now some possible solutions. Joyous, she could not wait to journey back down this great mountain and call her dear friend Michael.

First, though, she had to make a copy of her summary notes on Charlie's printer and ask him to drive to Lily's apartment and ask her to deliver the copy to her dear friend Zachary. Fila later heard back that Zachary was 100% delighted and could not wait to get back to visit with her again.

"Fila, Fila, slow down, you are so excited, said Michael. "Look, rewrite everything you are trying to tell me very clearly and have your friend Charlie there, or Lily, mail it to me. You said these are just outline thoughts and that we could work together to fill in the blanks. I want to do that. As you know I'm not in Denver anymore. Here, let me give you my new address."

"Oh Michael, thank you, thank you. I feel so relieved now. I want to do some good with my life now after what I did six years ago on 9/11. I know you have great influence. I…"

"We have the same goal, Fila," Michael interjected softly. "We are going to try to get this thing done. Yeah I know America has drug overdose deaths, viral infection deaths, and car accident deaths all adding up into the many thousands per year, but violence bugs me too. We lost twenty million people 9/11, six percent of our population, and incredible suffering for a long time in getting food and water to the survivors…." He paused, and Fila was silent.

Many seconds passed. "Michael, I…"

"Don't say anything. I know your story from your time as a child. I'm not blaming you. I still want you to come back. You are in hiding there. I can make it better here with me…"

"Not yet Michael, not yet, let me think. I need time. Please."

And so it ends. The summer of 2027. No one knows the story in the Roaring Fork Valley the next three years.

Twenty-two

September 11, 2030

Alex was still sitting perfectly still, his eyes and mouth wide open, listening intently to his father's long story. The stately room was dimly lit, but warm and soft. It was quiet all about. Michael had now stopped talking, simply gazing out at nothing. It was getting quite late for a ten year old, but he felt no tiredness, only intrigue. His dad had paused for a long time after the telling of the written messages he had received from Fila in 2027, three years before.

"Dad, dad, is that it? That's the end? Look, Aunt Alexis became president again in 2028 and named you Vice President. They taught us in school how you were appointed by her to negotiate all the things Fila wanted done. And you did it! The world is safer. My teachers constantly praise you. Dad, we are safer. Fantastic, dad!" Even at this late hour, Alex could not contain his excitement. "And geez, like mom dying of cancer five years ago, and with Aunt Alexis also dying recently, you are now the president -- here we are sitting in the Oval Office, and **you are the President of the United States!** Dad, you have done it....

"But I care about you too, dad, and what you have told me about her. I feel her. I know you must love her. Call her. Please. Tell her that. Bring her back to us. Dad!"

EPILOGUE

O ver these last ten years, it has been the author's intent in writing this trilogy to, yes entertain readers with fictional characters and suspenseful events, but more importantly to bring more attention to matters of national importance. The first concerns the grave matter of climate change where the planet has been in a gradual overall warming phase the last some one hundred years. My point being that rather than we jump to extreme conclusions and countermeasures including blaming man, we perform more and better Research into this complex field understanding the principle that ' **the science is never done**'. So we still really have to figure it all out. Hence, *A Truthful Myth*. At the same time going forward, we need to introduce innovative methods to Adapt to changing climates and to invent more ways to Mitigate against adverse impacts. Lastly, we should aim to better Prepare for future manmade and natural catastrophes sure to occur. In other words, RAMP Up.

Secondly, the author understands the general populace in going about his or her daily life does not think much about bad things that might occur within our country in the future. It's not our nature. But they do happen. Pandemics! The 2020 Covid 19 virus. So obviously, constitutionally, it is up to **our government** to think about these potential events and always plan to protect our security. WMD's. Number 1 priority. *In Three Days* portrays an attack on America with two weapons of mass destruction and an intentional epidemic. This is not science fiction.

The third and last concern of national importance that I write about is the matter of violence. A short book, *Sopris,* but one centered on an issue that has bothered me my entire life. Seven years old in 1945 listening to the radio of the surrender of the Japanese and the spontaneous joy around me. But the gruesome movies of the war, then incessant cowboy movies of the good guys shooting the bad guys, even the Disney stories always the evil villain and the good guy or girl, the entertainment world with its ever increasing scenes of graphic violence, the promise of the United Nations in the late '40's, but then the Korean War, the Cold War threat and nuclear weapons proliferation, Vietnam War, 9/11, al Qaeda, Iraq, Afghanistan, Syria, Taliban, ISIS, daily gun violence with innocent inner city kids dying, and on and on. So in *Sopris*, we have my main character named Fila, living with evil, seeking peace, turning evil, becoming good again – her ongoing conflict for why we are as we are – our human behavior good and bad. Maybe I leave in this story some good reasons for why we humans can be both competitive to the level of violence or conversely be cooperative to the advancement of our common good. But more importantly, in order to reduce violence perhaps some ideas future leaders can expand upon and prayerfully implement."

Printed in the United States
By Bookmasters